# CHILDREN OF STRANGERS

## BOOKS By LYLE SAXON

FABULOUS NEW ORLEANS

OLD LOUISIANA

LAFITTE THE PIRATE

FATHER MISSISSIPPI

CHILDREN OF STRANGERS

With Robert Tallant and Edward Dreyer

GUMBO YA-YA

# Children of Strangers

By
LYLE SAXON

**PELICAN PUBLISHING COMPANY**
GRETNA 1989

First published by Houghton Mifflin Company 1937
Published by arrangement with Houghton Mifflin Company
   by Robert L. Crager & Co. 1948
Published by arrangement with Robert L. Crager & Co.
   by Pelican Publishing Company, Inc. 1989

Pelican paperback edition
   First printing, September 1989

**Library of Congress Cataloging-in-Publication Data**

Saxon, Lyle, 1891-1946.
   Children of strangers / by Lyle Saxon. -- Pelican paperback ed.
      p.  cm.
   "First published by Houghton Mifflin Company 1937"--T.p. verso.
   I. Title.
PS3537 .A9756C4   1989                    89-3842
813' .52--dc 19                           CIP
ISBN 0-88289-397-1

Manufactured in the United States of America
Published by Pelican Publishing Company, Inc.
1101 Monroe Street, Gretna, Louisiana 70053

ALTHOUGH this book describes a real community in Louisiana, the characters are entirely fictional, and if any similarity is found to any living person it is purely coincidental.

Despite its simplicity, the story has been in preparation for several years, and fragments of it have appeared in *The Dial* and *Century Magazine*. The scene at the negro church has been rewritten from a story which appeared in the *New York Herald Tribune,* and the sermon is a real one taken down in a backwoods negro church on Easter morning.

Moreover of the children of the strangers that do so-journ among you, of them shall ye buy, and of their families that are with you, which they begat in your land: and they shall be your possession.

*Leviticus* **25:45**

# CONTENTS

# PART ONE

## *EASTER*, 1905

# CHAPTER I

FOG covered Cane River. The plantation was drowned
in a milky cloud that lay along the face of the earth. A
negro man in faded blue overalls stood on the river
bank holding a silver watch between his forefinger and
thumb, watching the last few minutes of sleeping-time
as they ticked away. When the hands of the watch
pointed to five o'clock, he sighed and began to ring the
plantation bell. Only the rope was visible to him, a rope
stretching up into the mist, and it seemed that the voice
of the bell should be muffled in the fog; but the sound
was silver clear as it rolled out over the invisible fields.

The first note of the bell went languidly across the
narrow river, quickened into an echo and rolled back,
meeting the next note midway of the stream. Now it
seemed that there were two bells ringing, mingling their
notes, separating, tangling together again, as each

measured tone was broken by its jangling echo. The sound of the bell swept across the fields, waking the negroes in their cabins; sleepy black men groaned and turned in their beds, and black women, lying beside them, stretched themselves like cats, before rising to make coffee for their men. The sound of the bell went on, dividing, uniting again into an unbroken stream, rushing against the big-house of the plantation, flowing around the white columns and penetrating the bowed green window blinds.

In his four-post bed the plantation owner yawned and opened his eyes to the bare, familiar room which held his boots and his guns, and which smelled of saddle-soap and leather. His black-and-white setter, sleeping on a deerskin rug beside the bed, beat sleepily upon the floor with his tail. In the adjoining room his wife woke and looked at the baby in a cradle beside her.

'Guy!' she called, 'there's the bell.'

His mother was awake, too. Across the hall the old lady lay like a woman of wax, her hair silver on the pillow; she put out a wrinkled hand and touched the red ribbon which marked the place in the Bible.

'Another day,' she said.

White men and black were waking up, gathering their strength, getting ready for a day of toil. The bell called them all. Even the animals understood. In the mule-lot a breath like a sigh swept up into the fog, as the mules turned their heads, all eyes looking in one direction, remembering yesterday's toil and waiting for to-day's harness.

The clangor of the bell went further and further, crossed the boundary of the plantation and roused Famie, a mulatto girl, who lay dreaming in her room on the old Vidal homestead.

Famie's eyes opened and she looked out through the open window. It was not yet sunrise. The weeping-willow trees were silver fountains in the mist and the dark masses of the fig trees were little gray hills. It was a still, cool day. Not a sound anywhere except the clamor of the bell; no bird called. Famie smiled into her pillow, happy in the memory of a dream of arms around her and a voice caressing her. As long as she made no effort to capture it, the dream hovered close, but as she attempted to hold it, it slipped away and was gone. Outside the window came a sudden flurry of flapping wings and the clear crowing of a cock; then a rustling of leaves as the chickens came flopping down from the fig trees. That old rooster had chased her dream away.

What was it that smelled so good? It must be ... must be ... She sat up in bed and leaned over to look. There it was, the first honeysuckle, a spray of creamy white flowers just under the window sill. She thrust out an arm, broke off the cluster and held it against her cheek. The leaves were wet with dew and a drop of water fell at the neck of her nightgown and ran down between her breasts. She laughed and shivered.

Her bare feet slipped to the floor and she crossed the room to look into the small mirror above the washstand. She peered at herself, standing there in her cotton nightgown, the honeysuckle in her hand. Her hair was ruffled, and she ran a slim hand through its dark waves. She was a woman now — sixteen years old today — and she could wear her hair on top of her head if she wanted to. She combed it up now to try the effect and wound the sprig of honeysuckle into the dark curls. No, that wasn't right, better comb it low on her neck. She tried it in that fashion, turning this way and that before the mirror. Finally she fastened it with a comb and let the honeysuckle droop down upon her shoulder. Now it was the gown that was wrong. She unbuttoned it and slipped it down, a falling-off-the-shoulder dress like a white lady at a ball. Yes, she was a woman now, and nobody, nobody in the world — unless he looked mighty close — could tell that she was a mulatto. There was a faint row of freckles across the bridge of her nose, as though she wore a spotted veil; the dreaming black eyes showed a thread of white beneath the pupil; her lips were very red and not too full ... No, she was like a Spanish girl, that was it.

She pulled the gown lower and caught it tight behind her with one hand so that her slender body was outlined, and turned, looking at herself from one side, smiling, showing her white teeth, and extending one arm toward the girl who smiled from the looking-glass...

The strokes of the bell became slower and slower, a pause, then one broken note as the clapper dropped back against the side of the bell.

A moment later she had thrown down the honeysuckle and had forgotten it. She was cold. She crouched by the fireplace where last night's embers still glowed beneath the ashes. A handful of fat-pine chips and dried moss was enough; there was a puff of white smoke and the blaze crackled up. With a gourd dipper she filled the smoke-blackened kettle and set it upon the flame, then rose to get the coffee-pot. She measured the coffee carefully, just enough for three people, and returned to crouch beside the hearth until the water boiled.

The room in its dimness seemed huge, with the old canopied bed with its faded red tester and four sturdy posts; the patchwork quilt was gay against the white sheet. A large table stood at the foot of the bed, and against one wall was a fine old sideboard with a black marble slab and brass claw feet. But the chairs were homemade, straight and simple with their seats of deer-hide and the smooth polish that comes only from years of use. The walls and the brick chimney-piece were whitewashed, but the ceiling was dark from the smoke of a century. It was all safe and familiar; it was home; she could remember no other room as her own; this had always been. And the old river was just eleven steps down from the back door.

She could still feel the rhythm of the bell, although it was silent now, and her thoughts flowed out, going, returning, vaguely, without conscious direction ... Last night in the moonlight on the river bank her cousin Numa had put his arm around her waist and had told her that she was beautiful, kissing her neck when she turned away her lips, begging her, pleading with her to love him ... Maybe, after awhile ... but Numa was more like a brother than a lover; she had known him so long and so well. A lover ought to be somebody from far off, tall and strong and different ... The moon had been white and Numa had brought her a white rose and her dress had been white in the dark shade of the tree ... Her grandmother had called her to come inside, saying it wasn't right for her to sit out there in the dew and catch her death of cold, maybe, with that good-for-nothing Numa. But the old woman's voice had been kind, for she liked Numa and expected Famie to marry him some day ... Not now, though, because she was still a girl at school ... School, and the nuns in the sunny rooms at the convent across the river, where yellow and brown and cream-colored children droned their lessons like sleepy bees, and where Famie's needlework was praised by Sister Désirée. Sister Désirée had skin like the paper in an old book. She was old now and sometimes cross; but she petted **Famie** and talked with her about holy things, as they sat in the grape arbor at recess time. Sister Désirée was good, but she was like a woman in a tale; she didn't seem real like other people. She talked in a hushed voice about the Holy Virgin and the Immaculate Conception and the baby Jesus. The Virgin Mary was not like other people either, and she hadn't sinned the sins of the flesh ... Not many people like that nowadays ... Famie smiled to herself, remembering her cousin Nita — the bad one — who got heavy penances from Father Broussard. The priest was old and stern, and when Famie went to confession she was afraid, stumbling over her words and talking so low that the priest would scold and tell her to talk louder. But she hadn't been obliged to confess bad things as Nita had ... There! The water was boiling.

In a few moments the aroma of coffee filled the room. Famie gathered three cups, a tray and the sugar bowl and brought them to the hearth. When enough coffee had dripped, she picked up the coffee-pot and the tray and went barefoot across the room and opened a door.

It was dark in there; the batten blinds were closed and the room smelled of old people in bed. Famie put down the tray and opened the wooden shutter of the window. The mound under the bedclothes stirred and a woman's voice came muffled through the sheet: 'Famie?'

'Here your coffee, *Marraine*.'

Her grandmother sat up in bed; she was dark and

round, and she looked like an old Indian woman. She patted the bedclothes with her hand and spoke in French: 'Wake up— old man. It's big daylight. Here's your coffee, Bizette.'

The grandfather emerged, thin and toothless, with his hair and beard very white against his yellow skin. He smiled and looked like a friendly old bird, and the hand that he put out for the cup was wrinkled, like a bird's claw.

'What! No wine?' he asked. He said this every day; it was his little joke.

Famie sat down upon the side of the bed and they drank together. The fog was rising and the gold sky was showing beyond the river. They spoke of the fog and of the trip to the plantation store that Famie and her grandmother were to make that day — simple things in the simple patois of the Cane River country.

The sun was shining in ribbons through the mist when Famie went back into her room. The fire had burned down to a bed of embers, so she added to it, piling pieces of wood against the andirons so that they would burn slowly. She placed six flatirons in a row on the hearth, their smooth surfaces turned to the blaze; then the metal cylinders which fitted into the fluting-iron were placed among the embers to heat. A pile of rough-dried clothes lay in a basket behind the door, and while the grandmother was dressing herself Famie sprinkled them. By the time the old woman came in,

Famie had laid out the ironing-board and, still in her nightgown, was ready to begin.

It was a delicate business, for the clothes were the fine linen dresses of Mrs. Randolph's baby, over at the big-house at Yucca Plantation. For more than two hours the two women worked, placing their irons neatly, turning the creaking fluting-iron with delicate care so that the ruffles should be crisp yet soft. In the doorway, looking out toward the river, the old man sat in the sunshine eating cold biscuits and milk from a blue-striped bowl, adding sugar, tasting, stirring, smiling to himself. Finally he fell asleep and a yellow hen came and pecked at the bowl as she searched for crumbs.

As the sunlight grew stronger the river sent its reflections into the house; silver rippled upon the blackened beams of the ceiling and upon the whitewashed walls; a row of glasses on the sideboard glittered with brilliant points of light. Famie smiled and blinked her eyes, and sniffed at the sweet scent of honeysuckle as it came in the open window. The house smelled of freshly ironed linen, and of woodsmoke; it was a clean smell.

# CHAPTER II

BEFORE nine o'clock the ironing was finished and the clothes were folded away into a flat basket of woven oak strips. Famie and her grandmother made ready to go on one of their infrequent trips to the commissary. Usually the small son of a neighbor carried the finer pieces of 'Miss Adelaide's' laundry back and forth, but today old Odalie and Famie were carrying it themselves. They dressed carefully; Famie in a freshly ironed guinea-blue calico dress and sunbonnet, and the woman in a white sacque and sunbonnet, and with the inevitable black skirt of 'half-mourning.' As they stood in their doorway they could see the big-house rising above its trees not more than half a mile away. But the big-house at Yucca was remote, for all that. There are barriers far greater than distance: race and timidity and old, threadbare pride.

Together they walked between the furrows to their gate, the light basket swinging between them and above its swinging shadow on the ground. On one side, the river curved beside the curving road, and on the other side the fields stretched out, freshly turned. Slowly down the long furrows moved straining figures, the plowmen and the mules, coaxing the weary earth into renewed and reluctant fertility. Beyond the fields the far-away woods burned blue in the haze of distance.

The road went to the commissary, then around it in a gentle curve to the gate to the flower garden of the big-house. The commissary was like a large Noah's Ark painted white with green batten doors; its narrow gable projected into the road and a porch beneath the gable-end faced the road and river. The store gallery was the loafing place, the central spot where friends met, and where news was gathered and gossip spread. On the gallery were three rickety chairs, a pair of scales and two rolls of barbed wire. This morning the double doors stood open, but the building was so dark inside that the interior was invisible from the road. 'Looks like night in there,' Famie said as they approached. Painted in the triangular gable-end was a faded sign: GUY RANDOLPH, and slightly below it, YUCCA PLANTATION STORE, and still lower the two rather mysterious words, GENERAL MERCHANDISE. An old china tree stood at one end of the gallery and to its trunk were tied a horse and a mule. The horse was a beautiful roan animal with a shining saddle — Mr. Guy's own saddle horse — and its presence signified that Mr. Randolph was in the store at the moment and not riding over the fields with the overseer. The mule had neither bridle nor saddle and was tied with a piece of heavy rope; across his back lay a folded gunnysack.

Three brightly dressed negro women loitered on the commissary steps. Their heads with yellow and blue bandanna *tignons* were close together and their attention seemed centered upon a small black girl who approached from the opposite direction, lackadaisically, her rags fluttering about her skinny legs, a coal-oil can swinging in one hand.

'Howdy, Miz Mug!' she piped in a shrill voice to one of the women who watched her approach.

Immediately the three women began to question her, all speaking together:

'What's all dat screamin' down de road?'

'Who was dat a-yellin' at yo'?'

And as the girl stood scraping one bare foot against the other, Mug cried out: 'Answer me, gal, don' yo' stan' wid yo' mouth open!'

The girl switched her skirt and answered pertly:

'Dat was Miss Crazy-Susie a-yellin'.'

'What she yellin' about? What she say?'

'She jus' come a-runnin' out de do' a-yellin' at me, an' she say a hog got in de house an' et up all her corn-meal — an' den she screech some mo' ...'

'What else she say?' cried the chorus.

'An' she say her daughter Ma'y goin' tuh have a baby an' *nobody* don' know who de pappy is. An' den she go on a-screechin'...'

'Do Jesus!'

'Gawd knows!'

'Hab mussy!'

'An' den she say dat her husban' done slap her down an' lef' her dis very mawnin'...'

'Lawd-Gawd!' cried the women in unison.

'An' den she fall down de flo' a-yellin' dat she don' believe in Gawd, no ma'am, nor Jesus neither!'

'Hab mussy!'

'Lissen tuh dat!'

As the girl seemed to have reached her climax, the women inquired: 'An' what yo' say to her, gal?'

The child replied in her vacuous, shrill voice, 'Ah jus' say: "Ah don' keer!"'

At this unexpected answer, the three women abandoned their simulated horror and burst into guffaws.

'Lawdy Gawd!'

'Now Jesus!'

'Great Day!'

'Dat's a crazy chile!'

The little girl, greatly pleased with herself, went flouncing into the store, and the women followed, pummeling each other, whooping with laughter.

Famie had lingered, listening, but she felt a sudden

tug at the basket. Her grandmother was staring straight ahead, her nostrils distended in scorn: 'Niggers!' she said. 'That's all they got to do, laughin' at a crazy woman!'

Famie tried to understand her grandmother's distaste, failed, and, watching a red bird's flight across the road, she forgot the incident at once. Together they went on, through the gate and up the path through the flower-garden, to the big-house.

Framed in greenery, the house rose before them. How big it was! The six white columns which supported the roof were enormous, and the galleries were large, too. A negro girl who was sweeping the lower gallery with slow, lazy strokes dropped the broom where she stood and languidly asked their business. Odalie indicated the basket and said that she wanted to talk to Miss Adelaide. Without another word the black girl went up the stairway which rose at one end of the porch. Famie and her grandmother waited, listening to the plop-plop of the girl's feet as she went along the upper gallery. A moment later she called down:

'She say tuh come up heah!'

They began their ascent, Famie stepping warily around the broom to avoid bad luck. The clothes-basket bumped against their legs on the stairway.

The planter's wife lay in a four-post bed in a front room on the upper floor, a bed so large that it occupied nearly one quarter of the big room. Beside her, upon the counterpane, lay the baby fresh from his bath and as naked as the day he was born. In one pudgy fist he grasped the end of his mother's long braid of brown hair.

'Look, Odalie,' Miss Adelaide said. 'He holds tight to everything he gets his hands on; he'll be rich some day.'

She laughed at the familiar superstition, and Odalie smiled, her face falling into many tiny wrinkles. An old black woman with a checkered head-handkerchief smiled grimly and said:

'Ain't yo' shame, Miz Adelaide? Po' li'l man is buck-naked befo' comp'ny,' and she lifted the child, swathed him in a pink blanket and carried him from the room.

Miss Adelaide looked at Famie who stood, smiling shyly, just inside the door:

'Who's that you've brought with you, Odalie?'

'That's my gran'chile, Euphémie Vidal. Come speak to Miz Ran'off, Famie.'

Miss Adelaide was plantation-raised, and she put the girl at her ease at once by the use of her nickname: 'How do you like my baby, Famie?' she asked.

'He's the prettiest li'l baby I ever *did* see,' the girl replied, and added, 'He's so lovely white.'

The white woman understood at once that wistful word. White. Yes, that's what they all wanted, poor things. Mulattoes, neither one thing nor the other.

'Aunt Dicey will bring him back as soon as he's

dressed,' she said. 'Now, Odalie, let's look at his clothes.'

While they were examining the laundry, Famie looked about the room. It was beautiful, she thought, as her eyes turned from white wall to white woodwork, to the yellow-and-white flowered curtains, and to the white matting on the floor. The tester of the bed was lined with yellow silk and there were yellow glass bottles on the dressing-table. Even the washbowl and pitcher had a band of yellow, and ... Famie gasped, startled, for there she was, herself, reflected full length in the mirrored door of the wardrobe. She saw herself as though for the first time, a slim, eager girl with black eyes and parted red lips, her pale face framed in the blue sunbonnet. She stared.

A sharp grunt of disdain brought her to herself, and beyond her shoulder, reflected in the glass, she saw the ironic smile of the old black woman who carried the baby in her arms. Famie flushed and turned away. Luckily, Miss Adelaide had noticed nothing, and as the girl approached the bed again the white woman spoke kindly to her.

'Your grandmother tells me that this is your birthday, and that you've been saving your laundry money for a new dress for Easter. I was wondering if I didn't have something that you would like. I'd like to give you a present, for Odalie tells me that you did all of this lovely fluting. It's beautiful, and nobody on the plantation can do it half so well.'

Then she spoke to the old black woman: 'Aunt Dicey, give me the baby, and open the *armoire* for me.'

The nurse placed the child upon the counterpane again and advanced to the wardrobe and opened its door; the mirror swung out and in its reflection the whole room seemed turning about. A sweet scent of *vertivert* filled the room.

'Look, Famie, you're taller than Aunt Dicey, see if you can reach down that hatbox from the top shelf ... That's right. Bring it here.'

Inside were three hats, piled one on top of the other. One was a big, floppy white leghorn with a bunch of red poppies at one side of the crown and, oddly enough, one poppy sewed under the brim.

Miss Adelaide turned it about in her hands: 'Would you like this?' she asked.

Famie caught her breath: 'For me?'

'Of course, who else?'

'Yes, *ma'am!*'

Miss Adelaide tossed it toward her: 'Here, take it. It's yours. Try it on and let's see how you look.'

Famie put aside the sunbonnet and placed the hat on her head.

'No, that's not right ... Come here and I'll show you,' and Miss Adelaide, with a deft touch settled the hat correctly with the single poppy bobbing near the girl's left cheek. Now Famie could look in the mirror unashamed; but she had had her lesson. One glance was enough. The hat was a miracle; she had never dreamed of having one so fine. She took it off again and held it in her hands as though it were a bird about to fly away.

Miss Adelaide appeared to forget all about the hat and began asking questions about Odalie's sister, old Madame Aubert Rocque, the oldest and most revered mulatto woman in the settlement on Isle Brevelle. 'Tell her to come and see my new baby. I went to see *her* when she was sick.' Miss Adelaide sounded brisk and gay.

A few minutes later the girl and her grandmother were going down the garden walk, the hat swinging in the basket between them.

'Now we got to go to de sto',' the old woman said.

The store was dark and smelled of salt meat and kerosene. Saddles and harness hung from the rafters; there was a pile of bright plow-points just inside the door; glass cases held men's hats and shiny shoes. Shelves on one side held groceries, and there were sacks of flour and cornmeal piled up in the middle of the floor. The clerk, a blond, fat, pimply young man stood playing idly with a pair of scissors and a skinny black woman was fingering a piece of checked material. Behind the clerk the shelves were piled with bolts of gay cotton cloth.

'Yo' wait on dem while I makes up my min',' the

woman said; then turning, 'Howdy, Miss Odalie, how yo' do?'

It was Lizzie Balize, the granny-doctor. Odalie thanked her for her courtesy, then turned to the clerk. It was hard to decide upon the proper material for Famie's dress — not that there was such a wide choice, but because a new dress is such an event that one must never, never make a mistake. Famie fingered the sprigged muslins and the pink organdy, but they were not quite what she wanted. At last she saw it, there on the shelf, a bolt of white dotted swiss. That was exactly right, and within the price that she could pay. Her enthusiasm was so contagious that the clerk smiled at her and became gracious, and ended by giving her half a yard extra for *lagniappe*.

'I'll give you something pretty if you come here by yourself sometime,' the clerk said, too low for Odalie to hear. Then, not waiting for an answer, he turned away and began wrapping up the parcel.

'Law! I clean forgot the cotton and thread,' said Odalie. It was true, for she had planned to make petticoats and chemises. The mistake was soon rectified, the money paid, and they made ready to go.

As the clerk handed Famie the fifteen cents in change, she felt his hot fingers pressing into her palm, and she moved away, startled. Odalie had not noticed, but Lizzie had missed nothing of the byplay: 'Humph!' she said, looking straight ahead of her.

It could mean anything, or nothing, but the clerk heard and his pasty face flushed. As Famie turned away she heard him say sharply,

'Well, Lizzie, make up your mind. I haven't got all day to fool with niggers.'

They were nearly home when they heard the clear note of a horn from the river. The girl dropped her bundles and ran through the house to look out at the back door. In the sunlit river a man with a wide straw hat was rowing a skiff, each dip of the oar sending out scores of shiny ripples. Standing in the stern of the boat a slim, mulatto boy blew blast after mellow blast from a conch-shell. The boy stood with his face to the noonday sun, his black curls glistening; he wore blue overalls and a red handkerchief was around his neck. As Famie watched, he put aside the shell, and cupping his hands to his mouth, he shouted:

> 'Fais Do-Do!
> Grande danse le soir de paques à huit heures!
> De la bonne musique, bon temps pour tous!
> Fais Do-Do!
> Au pavilion de monsieur Monette!
> Dimanche à huit heures. Ne manquez pas de venir!'

As puzzling as this sounded, it was perfectly clear to the girl who listened: old Monette was giving another party at his hall on Easter Sunday. There would be good music and everybody would be welcome. *Fais-*

*do-do*, meaning literally, 'Go to sleep,' was the local name for a dance.

Seeing Famie at the door, the boy in the boat pointed to her, then to himself, made a gesture of dancing, and stopped with arms extended. Famie turned and spoke to Odalie who stood at her shoulder: 'Numa say, can I go to the *fais-do-do* Sunday?'

The grandmother nodded, and Famie repeated the nod to the boy in the boat. He waved the conch-shell in pleased anticipation and blew another blast. Then, turning, he shouted the announcement toward the houses on the other shore. From the other bank came the clear call of a woman's voice, asking the hour when the dance would begin. The boy answered, then went on with his announcement. The boat moved slowly down the river, propelled with slow, even strokes. The note of the blown shell became fainter as the men went on their way. Famie stood looking after them, her hand pressed to her happy heart.

It was not long before the noon bell called the men from the fields. It was a glad sound, as though the bell itself was happy in calling the workers to rest. The notes were brassy and gay. Far afield men and mules heard it and were glad. Plows were abandoned where they stood; trace chains were released from the wagons; men mounted their mules and came at a quick trot down the lanes toward the barn. Now they were eager, laughing, joking with each other. One man was singing, another whistled. The chains jingled and the reverberation of the trotting hooves was like faraway thunder.

When the noonday meal was finished, the old man went to take a nap. He was feeble now and he was getting childish, but his temper and his affection were unvarying. Famie loved him with the quiet affection that one gives to a long-familiar object, a warm quilt, an old easy-chair. Her grandfather, like the house, had always been hers.

Odalie and Famie sewed all afternoon. The thin white cloth was spread out and cut according to pattern. They worked deftly, quickly, and the dress was half-finished before sunset. And as they worked they discussed in detail their trip to the store and the big-house. Half a dozen times, Famie laid aside her needle to try on the hat again. No one on Cane River had ever seen Miss Adelaide wear it; it was a miracle out of nowhere.

At sunset Famie stood holding the skirt — now basted together — against her body, watching its soft folds as they fell almost to the floor. Her cheeks were flushed; there were pins in her mouth. Odalie knelt beside her, adjusting a ruffle at the hem. From where she stood, Famie could see out through the side window. Her grandfather was working in the garden; he sang as he hoed, and the girl, looking, smiled to herself.

When the old man called the chickens, the women put aside their work and went to the window to watch.

He stood beside the well, a rusty pan cradled in the crook of his left arm; his right hand described a slow half-circle as he made ready to throw the first handful of grain. He was absorbed and intent. His call had in it the quaver of age:

'Hey, chick, chick, chick. . . . Hey, chick!'

Immediately there came a vast whirring of claw and wing as the chickens came like feathers blown in a great wind.

'Hey, chick, chick, chick . . . Hey, chick!'

The sun was setting and the colors were beginning to fade; the quick-falling night was coming.

Then from across the river came the pealing of the bell from the Catholic Church — a smooth, singing tone that called not to work, but to prayer. It was the Angelus. At once the woman and the girl folded their hands and bowed their heads. Famie could see the chickens standing in a circle, their heads turned expectantly upward. The old man stood motionless, a handful of grain arrested in a half-completed gesture. His eyes were closed and his lips moved as he stood with his face turned toward the evening sky.

Numa came in while they were still at the supper table. He had walked the mile from his father's house to bring a packet of Easter-egg dye to the old man. That was the reason that he gave, and old Bizette was pleased; but Famie knew that he had come to see her and she smiled at him in the lamplight. When the supper dishes were cleared away, they boiled a dozen eggs which the grandfather had gathered. They were all like children as the egg-dyeing progressed.

Some of the eggs were dyed a solid color, rich purple, arsenic green; but others received special care, for these dyes that Numa had brought were unlike any that they had seen before. There were bits of colored paper which, when applied to an egg and pressed with a vinegar-soaked cloth, produced astonishing results. Birds and flowers appeared. Easter rabbits. They crowded about the lamp, pleased, admiring. They were sorry when it was all over. That Numa! He was so good, so thoughtful, and he found it necessary to explain half a dozen times that he had ordered the dyes from the mail-order catalogue, weeks ago, in anticipation of this night. Old Bizette said again and again that no other old man at church on Easter would have such fine eggs.

Later Bizette sat alone at the table, polishing each egg with a greased cloth. Odalie went to her room to say her beads, and Numa and Famie went outside in the cool dark and sat on a bench under the china tree. The quiet river reflected the stars and the air was sweet with the scent of new-turned furrows.

His arm was around her, her head on his shoulder, and for a time they sat watching the starlit river. They were tired and happy, Famie lost in some vague dream, and Numa happy because he was beside her, touching her. But as her nearness stirred his desire, his arm tightened around her, and he turned her face toward him, kissing her eyelids, her cheek, then pressing his lips to hers. It was the first time she had let him kiss her mouth, and his passion communicated itself to her. For a moment she returned his kiss, forgetting that this was her familiar friend and sensing only his aggressive maleness. His breath came fast and his face, cupped between her hands, was hot. His hand tightened upon her breast. In the darkness she could feel him trembling against her: 'Famie, Famie...' he repeated, then, 'Love me, Famie. Now. I can't wait...'

There was a faint sick scent of fever on his breath. She drew away from him.

'No, Numa, no...Let me go. You mustn't!'

She pushed his hand from her breast and sat up. He moved toward her, trying to take her in his arms again.

'Ah, Famie...Famie...'

But the moment of ecstasy had passed. She sought to distract him:

'Look, Numa! Somebody's making a fire across the river.'

'I don't care nothin' about that. I want you.'

The fire flared bright on a wooded point a quarter of a mile away. The trees near it began to take on a ruddy glow, and the reflection of the blaze crossed the still river to their feet. Numa turned his head and looked at it, and Famie slipped from him. When he turned to her again, she was standing demurely, smoothing her skirt. And again came realization that although he loved her she did not want him as a lover. She was trying now to put him away from her. The understanding was bitter.

The fire now illuminated the river and the trees on the bank; the figure of a man was visible against the flames.

'What is it?' she asked. 'There's no house there. Who you think it is, Numa?'

His shoulders sagged, and his voice was hoarse as he answered, 'I don't know, Famie. Campers, I reckon.'

# CHAPTER III

BY NOON on Thursday the white dress was finished and laid away in the *armoire*. Famie stood looking out at the clouds which obscured the sun; but she knew that it would not rain. For on Holy Thursday the Virgin Mary and all the saints wash their robes for Easter and hang them out to dry. Somewhere up there, unseen by mortal eyes but clearly visible to all heaven, those celestial garments were flapping in the sunshine: 'I sho' wish I could see 'em!' she said to herself.

Early that morning her grandmother had removed the andirons and poker from the fireplace, for on Holy Thursday and Good Friday, iron and fire must not meet. Nor would the old woman permit a chicken, or any living thing, to be killed on those days — for to do so was to invite sure disaster. Odalie's sister had once killed a hen on Good Friday — and although she had done so absent-mindedly, having forgotten the holy day, every dish in her house had been broken before the year was out. Wasn't that enough to convince anybody?

There were many small tasks to be done in these last days of Holy Week. The few keepsakes from Famie's mother were taken from the *armoire*: a gold locket, a statue of a girl holding a dog, a pink lace fan with ivory sticks, a small gilt clock which had long ceased to run. These were souvenirs which remained from the light-hearted girl who had died in giving birth to Famie. Throughout the year they remained locked away in the dark wardrobe, but at Easter they were brought to the cemetery and placed upon her grave. This had been the yearly custom since her death. From Famie's father there remained but one relic, a rakish black felt hat which each year was laid among the flowers on his tombstone.

Other things were brought out and examined: six yards of black cotton cloth, and six yards of white. Year after year this material was festooned from grave to grave in the family plot, where it remained from Good Friday until the evening of Easter Monday. Then it was folded away until All Saints' Day. Many of the mulattoes followed this old custom and some of the trinkets left for several days in the cemetery were of real value; but never within the memory of the oldest man had anything been stolen from a grave.

The negroes were shouting Baptists and did not ob-
serve these customs of the mulatto Catholics. They
even plowed the ground on Good Friday, and, as a little
girl, Famie had been afraid to look into the new-turned
furrows for fear of seeing drops of the sacred blood of
Jesus in the broken ground.

Early Friday morning the girl and her grandparents
rowed across the river to the white church which stood
in a grove of trees nearly opposite their house. They
went to 'make their Easter' — to confession and to
decorate the graves. There were old women in the cemetery, bent on a similar mission. These were relatives and
friends, and they talked together as they bustled about,
sweeping cedar twigs and bird-droppings from the
graves, washing and filling vases in preparation for the
fresh flowers they had brought with them.

The smaller graves were gay with dolls and marbles
and tops; one had a green kite fluttering on the small
headstone. These were brought here at Easter to assure
the dead children that they were not forgotten.

The oldest graves had iron crosses, leaning this way
and that; others had marble headstones, or boards
painted white with black lettering. Epitaphs were in
French. There were bead wreaths and immortelles.
Some of the graves were decorated in shells, others were
outlined with bottles set upside-down in the earth.
There were a few box-like white tombs. The largest,
quite near the church, contained the remains of Great-

great-grandfather Augustin, who had owned all this part of the country a hundred years ago. He was the ancestor from whom the majority of the mulattoes had inherited their land. Old Augustin had owned a vast plantation on Isle Brevelle which he in turn had inherited from his father — a white man. Accordingly, *Grandpère* Augustin was their patriarch, one might almost say their patron saint. And although he had been dead for three quarters of a century he seemed familiar to all of them. His full-length portrait hung in the house of his granddaughter, Madame Aubert Rocque, and was so lifelike that Famie felt she had known him. He had donated the land for the convent, too, and for the church and cemetery, and he had built the first mulatto Catholic church. He had been rich, rich, but now he lay in the cemetery with all the others.

There were not many flowers, for spring was late this year; but upon nearly every grave the glass vases held red lilies or sprays of honeysuckle or clusters of pear blossoms. The vermilion of flowering quince was gay against brown earth and white tomb.

While old Bizette was in the church burning a candle to Saint Joseph, and making his prayer, Famie and Odalie decorated the graves in their family plot. The black-and-white cloth was draped from headstone to headstone, and tied in place with string. The vases were filled with flowers, and Famie arranged her mother's possessions neatly upon her grave: the pink fan, the gilt clock, and the statue were placed side by side. Upon her father's grave the black hat lay surrounded by a wreath of purple wistaria.

Odalie stood looking down upon the keepsakes which were gay in the sunshine, and Famie saw that her cheeks were wet with tears; she looked old and sad. Suddenly the girl was ashamed of her light spirits. For, no matter how hard she tried, she could feel no sorrow. She was only glad that the sun was shining and that she had a new dress for Easter. Death was for old people; it had nothing to do with her.

Their task finished, they turned to the church. At the door they met Famie's cousin Nita — the bad one — coming out. She kissed Odalie and smiled ruefully at Famie, then sat down upon the steps and rubbed her slim legs.

'Father Broussard sho' did me bad this time,' she said. 'He give me a *long* penance. Um! I been on my po' knees for mo' than two hours!'

'How you feel now?' Famie asked.

'Oh, I feel fine inside,' Nita answered, 'but my legs are plum broke down.'

The church smelled of wax candles burning. Famie dipped her forefinger into the holy-water font and made the sign of the cross. Then with a genuflexion toward the altar, she approached the confessional.

Nita was still standing on the steps when Famie came out, and the two girls walked into the churchyard together and sat down under a cedar tree. They were a little shy with each other, but until recently they had been classmates at the convent, where Nita had played Famie many a sly trick.

At first they talked of the *fais-do-do* on Easter night, and Famie told proudly of her new dress and hat: 'It's jus' the pretties' thing you ever *did* see.'

And then, after a silence, she spoke of the thing that had been troubling her:

'Nita, I got something I want to tell you and ask you 'bout.'

The other girl looked at her. 'What's the matter? Have you got into trouble with Numa?'

Famie laughed: 'No, Nita, I ain't like you.'

'I'll bet a man's got something to do with it,' the other said, unabashed. 'Hurry up and tell me. *Tante* Odalie'll be here an' you won't get a chance.'

Famie looked over her shoulder to make sure that they were alone, then lowered her voice: 'Nita, do you know that white man that clerks in the sto'?'

'What!' Nita's voice came quick and sharp. 'A white man? You mean ol' man Jennings?'

'No. He's gone off somewheres, and Mr. Guy's got a new clerk now. He looks like a hill-man to me. I never did see him befo' I went to the sto' with *Marraine* Tuesday. He's a kind of youngish man, 'bout twenty-five and he got yellow hair.'

'I don't know him,' Nita said. 'Why you so interes' in him, Famie, what he do?'

Famie told of the clerk giving her the extra half-yard of cloth for *lagniappe,* and of his whispered invitation to come back to the store alone some day. Nita's eyes opened wide as she listened.

'An' when he give me my fifteen cents change, he kind of run his finger into my hand an' pressed it. It pure scared me,' Famie ended.

Nita whistled soundlessly: 'Did yo' grandma see him do that?'

'No, she didn't see, but Lizzie Balize — you know, old Lizzie the granny-doctor — she saw him, an' she grunted plum out loud. I sho' was scared. But *Marraine* never saw nothin' at all ... an' I never told her, neither.'

Nita seemed lost in thought for a moment. Suddenly she grinned and asked: 'Did you confess that to Father Broussard, just now?'

'Why, of co'se not, Nita. The idea! It wasn't nothin' to confess. I didn't do a thing.'

'I was jus' foolin', Famie.'

She looked across the churchyard, her eyes half-closed, while Famie watched her, feeling half sorry that she had confided her secret. But after all, Nita knew all about things like that, and could tell her what the white man meant.

'If I was you, I'd sho' let him alone. You don't know nothin' 'bout him, and those hill-mens is likely to get you into a peck of trouble. I'm tellin' you what I know. You'd better keep away from there ... An' besides' —

she had just thought of something else — 'if Lizzie saw him playin' with yo' hand, she's goin' to be on the watch-out, an' if you *do* go there, she's goin' to talk about you as sho's you're born. Yes suh! She'll hang yo' name on every gatepost!'

'But Nita . . . I ain't goin' back. I jus' wanted to ask you what you thought . . .'

'I'm tellin' you what I think. I'd sho' keep away from there. If Mr. Guy ever foun' out that you was foolin' wid his clerk, there ain't no tellin' *what* might happen.'

Famie was astonished. Why was Nita talking like this? Usually she was so daring. Often she had urged Famie to mischief, and she was so careless about her own reputation that it was difficult to believe this sage advice.

'Nita, you talk jus' like you was my gramma.'

The other girl laughed and stood up: 'I got to go,' she said. 'I'll see you at church, Sunday.' She took a step and paused, stooping to rub her knee. 'I declare, Famie, but Father Broussard is a mean ole man. My leg is so' as a boil from all that prayin'.'

Left alone under the leafy tree, Famie wondered more and more. She had been so sure that Nita would be excited, and had even thought that she might urge her to return to the store, or would offer to go with her to look at the new clerk. Maybe Father Broussard's penance had made her better. Yes, that must be it . . .

She was still pondering on Nita's reformation when her grandparents came out of the church.

# CHAPTER IV

NITA lost no time. She was smiling to herself as she hurried down to her boat, tied among the willow trees. She pushed it adrift and stepped lightly in. The paddle rose and fell with easy, practiced strokes. She was not going toward home, but downstream instead. A few minutes later she tied the boat and was hastening up the other bank toward the commissary. What a baby Famie was! What an innocent child!

The road was empty in the sun. There was no one on the store gallery, and Nita stopped for breath when she reached the steps, resting a little and gathering her forces for conquest.

The blond clerk was alone. He sat on the counter with his back toward her, reading a newspaper. Nita paused in the door, knowing that her thin dress would be nearly transparent to one inside. She turned and raised her arm as though she were taking leave of an imaginary companion:

'Good-bye!' she called softly. 'Write to me... What?' as though in answer to a question — 'Oh, my *ad*dress? Just Nita Vidal, at Yucca Plantation. Yes! I come here every week for my mail.'

She was still smiling into the empty road when she heard the rustle of a newspaper behind her. She turned and faced the clerk with a gasp of astonishment, her hand pressed to her heart.

'Oh, you scared me, suh! I didn't see you.'

The clerk licked his red lips: 'So you come here every week, hanh?'

Nita looked down and smiled. She knew that she would have a new dress for Easter now.

Three o'clock on Sunday morning.

Famie, lying awake in the moonlight by the window, heard the negroes on their way to sunrise service; their hushed voices came to her, and the galloping of horses, soft in the dusty road; at intervals she heard the creaking of a wagon or the rattle of buggy wheels. Every negro on the plantation was making his way to Saint Mary's, the church in the woods five miles away. Packed in the dark building they would sing and shout until the sun rose — a sun that danced for joy, they said, on Resurrection Day.

Something of their hushed excitement was communicated to her as she lay listening. She caught herself humming aloud, but stopped at once for fear of disturbing the old people in the next room. Finally she could bear inactivity no longer. She went barefoot to the back door. The river lay sleeping in the light of the westering moon, and the trees were blue against the water. Her heart fluttered as though a bird were inside; her body tingled and her face was hot as she pressed her hands against it. Why did she feel like this? Was it fever?

As she sat in the doorway her thoughts went to Numa's kisses, then to the white man in the store, of his red lips and his hot hand pressing against hers. It wasn't that she wanted to go back there, but something seemed to call her. Not Numa, no, and not the man in the store, but something ... someone ...

Beyond the river she saw a lantern moving among the trees. The man who was camping there was stirring already; maybe he was going fishing.

The moon was still shining, but in the east the sky was beginning to show gray.

The chill dawn gave place to a warm and windless day. The sun shone bright on Isle Brevelle and the leafy lanes were filled with people on their way to church; some rode in surreys or buggies or in creaking wagons; others came on horseback, and families who lived nearby came walking through the checkered shade, mothers with babies in their arms, fathers with small boys swinging to their thumbs.

Skiffs moved in and out among the willows at the river bank, and dark-eyed girls, coming up from the boats, paused at the top of the incline to shake out their starched dresses.

The grassy plot before the church door was filled with people, and groups were under the trees beside the cemetery wall. They were all subdued and quiet and seemed a little sad.

The boys and girls were handsome, their skins cream-colored or light tan, their features clear-cut, hair and eyes black, teeth white. Many could have passed for white persons. But the older men and women were of darker pigmentation; they seemed a delicate race of Latins which had lived too near the sun. Even the very old were curiously erect, their thin shoulders back, their chins up. They were sad, but they had dignity. Their voices were modulated and each sentence ended with a rising inflection as though they asked questions to which there were no answers.

Their French extraction was evident in the grace with which they wore their threadbare clothes; and there was something Latin in the family groups, a unity, a deference to age and relationship. Old people were surrounded by nephews and nieces and grandchildren. Their soft voices called to one another, sometimes in the Cane River patois, sometimes in English. Names were called, soft French names and diminutives:

'Eh, Suzanne!'

'Mélanie!'

'You lookin' good, *chère*.'

'You too, Anastazie!'

'So, it is you, Octave? How you been?'

'*Ça va bien. Et vous?*'

Girls called to each other. The air was filled with their musical names: Aline, Natalie, Odette, Clothilde, Marie, Cécile, Zéline.

Sunshine flickered on the starched gray calico of the old women and the white ruffles of young girls. The group under the trees was like an old picture that has faded with the years.

From the convent came eight nuns, walking in couples through the flickering sunlight, their black robes and veils vivid against green young leaves; their heads were bent over their breviaries as they came slowly down the dusty road. At the gate they put aside their books with a quick gesture and raised their heads as they approached the church. The group fell silent and parted to let them pass.

Famie and her grandparents came up from their rowboat just as the bell called the worshipers into the church. A group of young girls surrounded them, exclaiming over Famie's new dress and hat. The poppies seemed doubly red in the sun. Numa disengaged himself from a gathering of men and came up smiling. He too had new clothes for Easter, a white linen suit; Famie had never seen him look so fine. He put his hot hand on the girl's cool arm and spoke in a whisper: 'You look like an angel...' She laughed and put her hand in his.

Old Odalie smiled as she watched them going into the church door. They were like a bridegroom and a bride.

When Mass was over, the old men sat among the graves and spread their dyed Easter eggs upon the ground. Old Bizette, holding his purple egg in his brown fingers, challenged his eighty-year-old cousin Henri to a game of Nip and Tuck. Bets were made, nickels and dimes clinking down upon a tombstone. More than forty old men had brought eggs to church with them, and the game prolonged itself for an hour.

Numa stood by watching, awkward in his new suit, laughing in refusal when old Bizette offered to give him an egg with which to try his luck.

'Young folks don't have no fun, no,' the old man said. 'Why, when I was yo' age, I couldn't wait fo' Easter to come. Me, I won plenty money wid my aigs in my day!'

Another old man spoke: 'It's de truth, Bizette. Me, I remember sittin' right here, seventy years ago, watchin' *Grandpère* Augustin tuckin' aigs. I was little boy, 'bout six years old. Hey law!' He sighed and returned to his game, there in the shadow of Augustin's tomb.

Half a dozen small fires were burning near the ceme-

tery wall and women crouched over boiling kettles.
The coffee-drinking was about to begin and the air was
filled with the aroma of coffee and the scent of flowers.
People were gayer now; laughter was heard. Cups and
spoons clinked together.

Famie went from group to group looking for Nita, but
nobody had seen her.

Eight o'clock at night.

In Monette's palmetto-thatched pavilion two accordions and a triangle furnished the music for dancing.
Sometimes the triangle-player put aside his ringing
metal instrument and beat upon a drum; for it was to
rhythm that the mulattoes danced, and the accordions
furnished a superfluous but pleasing melody. The
music was slow and the couples moved slowly holding
each other close.

*Fais-do-do!* Go to sleep!

Outside the blue moonlight shone down upon the
rippling river, but inside the pavilion the smoking
kerosene lamps spread their yellow glow upon a row of
impassive old women seated along the walls. Lamplight
shone on their full, starched skirts, their red-and-blue
checked *tignons*, and upon their wrinkled yellow faces.
Their turbaned heads nodded and their palmetto fans
swayed in time with the languid drumbeats.

These were the mothers and grandmothers, and they
represented the old *régime;* they were the hawks that

guarded the doves, and they wore the traditional cos-
tume of the chaperone. But the young people knew
little and cared less for the old-time ways. The girls
were gay in flowered print dresses, or in white, and the
boys wore cotton trousers and shirts open at the throat.
None of the men wore a coat; few even owned one.

Old Monette sat on a high stool at the door, and as
the men entered, he took from each a twenty-five-cent
piece and stamped upon the back of his left hand the
word 'Paid,' using a rubber stamp and green ink. After
that the men were free to come and go as they pleased,
and they passed continually in and out of the pavilion.
From time to time Monette called a boy to examine his
hand; for sometimes one tried to cheat. It was an easy
matter to slip from the hall while the ink was still wet
and press the back of his hand to the hand of another
boy. The word 'Paid' was transferred to the other's
hand as well — but the lettering was reversed. From a
little distance this was hard to detect, but when Monette
discovered the rogue, he was ejected from the hall with
much laughter.

Beside Monette was a barrel of lemonade. A dozen
glasses shone on a white-scrubbed shelf. A drink cost
five cents, and the boys and girls came singly to buy.
No girl allowed a boy to pay for her refreshment; it was
the Cane River code. Nor did the girls leave the room
except in the company of an older woman, although
they went sometimes with boys to the end of the

pavilion behind the orchestra where lights were dim.
So much was permitted but no more.

Nita made a spectacular entrance, a new red silk
dress billowing around her, her black hair combed low
and parted, Madonna fashion, a white rose behind her
ear. She carried a large black fan, and her face was
pale with powder. She was accompanied by her older
sister, a scrawny, yellow woman with spectacles, who
promptly joined the chaperones by the wall.

The old women looked at Nita and whispered to each
other behind their fans. But Nita, the bad one, paid
not the slightest attention to them and was surrounded
by boys and young men at once, and by girls who came,
envious and curious, to examine her dress. She was
pleased with the sensation she created and danced off
at once to the renewed whine of the accordions and the
quick, identical notes of the triangle.

The drummer sang a song in which the accordion-
players joined:

> Ai-yi-yi!
> Ai-yi-yi!
> Let's go to Cloutierville!
> Ai-yi-yi!
> Ai-yi-yi!
> Let's see the pretty girls!

The song went on and on, ending with a different
line each time. It appeared that the singer wanted to
see the girls in every near-by village. Sometimes it was

a striped dress that he wanted to see; at other times it was a pair of black eyes or rosy cheeks. The song became a hypnotic chant with its monotonous reiteration. At last the singer began to improvise:

> Ai-yi-yi!
> Ai-yi-yi!
> She's got a red dress on.
> Ai-yi-yi!
> Ai-yi-yi!
> Nobody knows where she got it from!

Nita laughed, unembarrassed, but the women along the walls whispered again behind their fans. Monette spoke to the singer and the song ended with a rattle of the drum.

Famie and Numa arrived with Bizette and Odalie a few minutes later. The old couple joined their friends and Odalie's fan was soon swaying in unison with the others. Famie stood looking at the slow-twirling couples, her hand on Numa's arm, her pleasure in her own new dress dimmed before Nita's elegance. The dancing couples called out as they went past:

'Hey, Famie, you late!'

'Hi, Numa, where you been, boy?'

And they called back: 'Hi, Zéline! Hey, Célie! How you do, Baptiste!'

They were all there, Annette, Natalie, Eulalie, and the rest, all happy, all dancing, glad that Lent was over and that good times had come again.

Famie danced first with Numa, then with her cousin Denis, then with a slim boy called Ignatius. She went from one to the other, intoxicated with the rhythm of the music, the arms around her, the other body moving in unison with hers; she was a little dizzy and the lamps became blotches of light.

In an intermission she went to sit beside Odalie and to beg the loan of her fan. Beyond the opening in the wall she could see the black faces of negroes standing outside watching, drawn irresistibly by the music. Monette saw the black faces too, and spoke to one of the accordion-players who sat listlessly in his place, chair tilted back. At once the man smiled and began to play the accompaniment for a song and presently he began to sing. It was a familiar Cane River song of a father whose daughter had brought disgrace upon him. The chorus ended:

> I wouldn't mind the fellow
> If his skin was yellow,
> But Mary's run away with a coon!

When Famie looked again into the darkness outside, she saw that the negroes had gone. The insult of the song had done its work.

The smoking lamps filled the hall with the odor of kerosene. Ice clinked against the tin dipper as Monette filled and refilled the glasses. Outside in the cool dark the boys passed their flasks of corn whiskey from hand to hand. Monette went out once to stop a fight and returned triumphant, rubbing his hands.

Presently the music began again and the couples resumed the dance. It was gayer now, more abandoned. Along the walls the fans moved faster in time with the quickened rhythm.

Monette had been drinking and had grown more tolerant. The accordion-players began to sing along with their playing, this time improvising a couplet about old Madame Monette who had come upon the floor to dance with her husband:

> Ai-yi-yi!
> Ai-yi-yi!
> Ol' Madame Monette
> She dance an' she sweat!
> Ai-yi-yi!
> Oh, Oh, how she sweat!

There was a burst of laughter, and the old woman shook a fist at the singer in mock anger; he continued, growing bolder:

> Ai-yi-yi!
> Ai-yi-yi!
> She drink plenty wine,
> An' she stick out behine!
> Ai-yi-yi!
> Oh, what a behine!

Madame Monette stopped dancing and cuffed the singer with her open hand. Then handed him a glass of lemonade. The old women along the walls rocked with laughter: 'Now, people! She's a hard case!'

And the dance went on. The room grew warm, the smoking lamps filled the pavilion with their greasy smoke. There were cries and laughter. It was nearly midnight.

A strange man was leaning against a window frame drinking from a glass and talking with someone in the darkness outside. He was six feet tall and proportionately broad — an unusual thing among Cane River men. He stood near a lamp and the light fell upon his greased black hair and his shining teeth. His pink shirt was open and revealed his bare chest. When he had finished drinking, he put aside his glass and leaned against the wall, arms folded, watching the girls through narrowed lids, following them with his eyes, but not moving his head.

He looked at Famie and smiled a little, then touched Numa's shoulder:

'Eh, Christophe!' cried Numa. 'When you get back?'

'Who's that?' Famie asked.

Numa danced on, and after he had put the width of the hall between them and the stranger, he said:

'That's Christophe Monette. He's been off workin' in New Awlins. He jus' come home.'

'What he do down there?'

Numa shrugged his thin shoulders: 'I don' rightly

know, Famie, but it's somethin' funny, I'll bet. He's a plum rogue.'

'He's mighty good-lookin'.'

There was a pause in which they crossed the room again, then the boy said: 'Maybe he is, but he's too speedy fo' me. He's mo' Nita's class than yo's.'

Later, as Famie sat alone, draining a lemonade glass, Christophe approached and slouched into the chair beside her:

'What you been doin' to yourself, Famie? You're the pretties' girl on Cane River.'

They talked for a few minutes, while he recalled her as a small girl at the convent. He leaned close to her, his knee pressing against hers as he teased her about Numa. She looked at him, wondering why he seemed unlike the other boys. His trousers were tight and his shirt open far down the front; he looked naked under his clothes. She could smell the sweet pomade in his hair.

When she danced with him he held her tight against his bare chest and his knee was insistent against hers. In a dim corner he put his hot mouth against her throat, pressing his teeth into her flesh. She was startled and jerked free from his embrace, standing still, holding him off, her hand flat against his chest.

'Stop it! Let me alone!'

He laughed: 'What's the matter, afraid?' he taunted.

They resumed the dance, and he led her dextrously into the light again: 'I'm coming to see you late to-night,' he said.

'Yes, an' you'll get shot, too,' Famie said, taking the flippant tone that she had learned from Nita.

'All right, baby,' he said. 'If I can't get you, I'll get somebody else.' He laughed, and released her as the tune ended.

Nita and her partner were at Famie's elbow.

'Hello, Christophe!' said Nita. 'Where you been this long time?'

Famie saw Christophe's eyes looking through the red dress as though he were about to tear it away.

Nita smiled and plied her fan.

In the dilapidated surrey, as they rode home, Numa tried to kiss Famie, but she pulled away from him: 'I'm tired, Numa.'

Old Bizette clicked his tongue to the aged horse, and Odalie dozed beside him. Numa looked out over the dark fields, hurt and miserable. Famie still felt the beat of the music and thought of Christophe. She did not want him, but his touch had excited her.

She went to sleep in the dawn wondering how Nita got that red silk dress, but she dreamed of a man in a pink shirt with a bare chest. The man in her dream was not Christophe. His skin was white.

# CHAPTER V

THE Monday following Easter was a lazy day. Famie went about her household tasks in a dream, sighing sometimes, although she did not know why. No one came to the house, not even Numa, but she could hear the shouts of the negroes in the fields, and could see the plowmen moving along the furrows. When the bell rang at noon, she listened to the muffled thunder of the mules as they came trotting in and she placed the frugal dinner upon the table while the dust of their passing still hung over the road. In the afternoon, as she sat sewing in the doorway, she saw people passing on their way to the commissary and recognized the black sun-bonnet of Lizzie Balize. The woman was walking fast with her covered basket on her arm:

'Somebody mus' be sick down yonder,' Famie said to herself.

Twilight came and the evening meal was eaten. By black-dark they were all in bed. From her window Famie could see the camper's fire reflecting itself in the quiet river, and a man moving about under the trees. He had been there for nearly a week now. Tomorrow, on her way home from school, she would pass that way and look at him. She lay back on the pillow and composed herself, to sleep. Was he a white man? What was he doing there?

On Tuesday morning she rowed across the river to the convent school near the church. In the sunny rooms the cream-colored and brown children droned their lessons: six times two is twelve, six times three is eighteen. As usual they recited their prayers in chorus, hardly conscious of the meaning of the words: 'Hail-Mary-full-of-grace-blessed-art-thou-among-women-and-blessed-be-the-fruit-of-thy-womb-Jesus . . .'

The nuns moved about, hearing the lessons, setting copies for the exercise in writing: 'The Lord is my Shepherd, I shall not want.' On the wall was a chromo of the child Jesus, a woolly lamb in his arms.

At the noon recess Famie looked about for Sister Désirée, but learned that she was ill in her room, so she joined the group of larger girls who were eating corn-bread and syrup in the grape arbor. Some of them spoke of church the day before. Only one of the girls had attended the *fais-do-do*, and she had gone home early.

The conversation was all of a play that the younger girls were rehearsing. Famie felt that she was older and wiser than any of them. It was true enough, for the classes ended with the sixth grade and there were only a few boys and girls who completed even these. The older pupils came irregularly, for most of the boys plowed and the girls were needed at home. Famie herself had attended only at intervals, for last year there had not been enough money to pay the small sum necessary for tuition. Today she felt apart from the others, and was glad that two more months would see her done with it all. She was grown up now; she knew enough.

When school was over she went down to her skiff among the willow trees and set it adrift. She remained there in the slow-moving boat, undecided, lost in vague thoughts. She was thinking of the man who camped on the river bank, half a mile away; she was curious to see him. Strangers came so seldom to this quiet place. She hesitated, then took up the oars, drawn by an impulse that she did not name.

As she approached the inlet near the spot where she had seen the fire, she hesitated. Suppose the man were a tramp, or a criminal in hiding? Suppose he stopped her and asked her what she wanted? She was near the bank, and soon would round a small hillock covered with a Cherokee-rose thicket. If she stopped there she might be able to see without being seen.

A few strokes and she felt the boat nose into the jungle-like growth; the young willow trees closed around her, and her boat lay hidden beside the briary hedge. There was an opening as though prowling animals had made a path through. Famie stepped out of the boat, and, crouching, went slowly forward, holding her dress aside from the thorny vines which impeded every step. The hillock was narrow, and after half a dozen steps she saw light shining through a gap in the hedge. She crept on hands and knees to the water's edge, parted the vines and looked out.

She had crossed a small point of land which formed one side of a narrow inlet, and across the strip of sun-flecked water she could see a rowboat tied to a syca-more tree; behind it the ground rose sharply, and at the top of a wooded incline there smouldered a dying fire in a clearing, a spiral of blue smoke curling upward. Beside the fire lay a black-and-white spotted dog, his nose upon his crossed forepaws. Above the bushes she could see part of a small tent. So dense was the foliage that the inlet lay in shadow, checkered with bright spots of dancing sunlight.

The man was nowhere to be seen.

It was quiet there, only the lapping of the water and the soft bird notes; and from the far-off fields she heard a negro shouting to his mule. In her hiding place the girl waited, her hand pressed to her side as though to still the pounding of her heart. Soon she would creep back to her boat again.

Something rustled behind her and she turned, startled. A mocking-bird regarded her with small bright eyes, then flirted his tail and was gone.

When she looked across the inlet again, the man was standing in the sunlight on the path beside the fire. He was naked and his hair flamed red in the sun. His body was startlingly white against the green leaves. He stood motionless, facing her, and as she watched he yawned, both hands to his mouth, then stretched himself, standing on tiptoe, arms extended outward and above his head.

The girl behind the vines felt the quality of a familiar dream; it seemed to her that she had waited for this, had known that it would happen. She was held motionless as though weighed down with sleep.

The man stood flexing his muscles, then descended the path to the water's edge, moving lightly and without sound. As he stepped into his boat, he called to the dog: 'Here, boy!' Then he dived into the water leaving a circle of widening ripples. The black-and-white setter stood on the bank watching, one forepaw raised.

Famie cowered back into the thicket.

The man came to the surface quite close to her, blew the water from his mouth and brushed back his hair. Then he turned in the water, easily, and remained still, floating, his face to the sky. He was so near that the girl could see the fine red hair curling on his chest. She crouched watching him, her breath indrawn.

After a time he began to swim, calling for the dog to join him, and the dog sprang in with a splash. Swimming together was evidently an old game with them both, for they fought together in rough play. Now it was the dog's sleek head that was uppermost, now the man's wet red hair became brilliant in the glancing sunlight that came through the leaves.

This was her chance for escape, yet she waited, watching, as he swam out into the river with slow and easy strokes. And as she lingered, he turned and swam back toward her, the dog swimming after him.

He did not return to his boat, but pulled himself up on a half-submerged log only a few feet away. She could hear his labored breathing.

The dog came scrambling up the bank and Famie put her hand over her mouth to stifle a scream. The dog growled, then barked sharply. With a bound he was upon the girl, snapping at her hands as she tried to beat him off. The man stood knee-deep in the water, parting the vines to see what the dog had found.

'What the hell?'

The next moment he was standing over her, grasping her wrist with his wet hand: 'Are you spying on me?' His voice was rough as he jerked her arm. Drops of water fell from his hair upon the girl's face.

'Please, suh! Please...' She could say no more.
She felt his grip relax, but he still held her arm.

'Who told you to come here? Are you by yourself?
Who's back there waiting for you?'

He clipped his words, looking past her into the
thorny hedge. The girl made an effort and answered:

'I'm all by myself...'

She could see the blue veins in his arms, and looking
up she saw his face in profile, his nostrils dilated, as he
listened for a noise behind her. A long minute passed,
broken only by his heavy breathing and by the water
as it dripped from his hair upon her dress.

When he looked down at her again he spoke softly:

'You scared the hell out of me. Where did you come
from? You live around here somewhere?'

'Yes, suh. I live across the river...I was comin'
home from school...' She could not finish. Her throat
contracted and her eyes were full of tears.

The man stared at her, the tip of his tongue showing
between white teeth. His bright blue eyes were narrowed.

'Just a girl on her way home from school!'

'Yes, suh...'

Again a pause, then his face changed as he repeated:
'Just a little girl on her way home from school. That's
good.' And then, 'Just you and me, hanh? Like the
babes in the wood.'

Famie nodded, tears hanging on her black lashes as

she looked up at him. The dog had withdrawn and lay watching them.

Suddenly the man expelled his breath with a great sigh. He threw himself down beside the girl and took her in his arms without a word. At the touch of his wet lips she lost all volition. She made no resistance as he pulled her roughly to him, but lay as in a dream, hardly conscious, without thought or reason.

Near-by the dog lay watching, and birds, disturbed in their nests, chirped angrily. Then it grew still in the thicket.

# CHAPTER VI

'MY GOD, Famie, where you been?'

Odalie stood in the doorway, a lamp in her hand. In the rowboat in the dark water Famie dropped the oars from her nerveless hands and tried to steady her voice as she answered:

'I — I stayed across the river ...'

'I been nearly crazy. I been callin' you ...'

'Yes'm, I heard you from over yonder. I came quick as I could.'

'What's the matter? You sick? You hurt yo'-self?'

Famie did not answer at once, she was trying to fasten the boat, but her shaking hands made it difficult. At last she dragged herself up the eleven steps to the door. Odalie put the lamp on the table and looked at the girl's stained and muddy dress, her disheveled hair.

'Oh, you look bad, Famie. What's happened to my chile?'

'It ... it ... oh, *Marraine!*'

Sobs choked her. Odalie helped her to a chair.

After a while the girl said: 'A dog scared me. I fell down and hurt myself.'

'Did he bite you? Bad? Let's see.'

'No'm ... I hurt myself when I fell.'

Oh, if Odalie would only go away and leave her.

'I'm all right now,' she said.

Her fright for the girl's safety appeased, Odalie became querulous: 'You ought to be 'shamed, a big girl like you, cryin' 'bout a dog. What you doin' out so late? What kep' you till black-night? An' me worryin' 'bout you, an' sendin' po' ol' Bizette to hunt you. The ol' man's like to fall down hisself ...'

At last Famie reassured her and Odalie went into her room, still grumbling. Alone, the girl sat for a time at the table by the lamp, her hands in her lap, her wet dress clinging to her knees. After a little she rose and undressed, throwing her soiled clothes into a tub of water outside the door.

By the time Bizette returned from his fruitless search, Odalie had baked the cornbread for supper and had placed the syrup and milk on the table. Famie made a pretense of eating, counting the minutes until the old people would go to bed. She talked a little of a strange dog she had encountered on the river bank, inventing details. At last, driven to give a reason for her long absence, she said that she had been with Sister Désirée who was ill. She had forgotten the time. She did not realize how late it had grown. She was sorry. Anything to be done with it all and to be let alone.

When the old people went to bed, Famie put out her light and waited until their heavy breathing told her that they were asleep. Then she began to wash her clothes, moving quietly, listening from time to time for sounds from the other room. It was done at last, and then she bathed herself. When she had finished, she brought the candle to the looking-glass and held it up, as she looked at her reflection.

The figure in the mirror was that of a stranger, a woman with dilated eyes and with a red mouth that seemed different from the girl's mouth she remembered. She slipped on her nightgown, put out the candle, and crept into bed.

The waning moon was just rising above the trees across the river and Famie lay looking out across the water. As she watched she saw a spark of flame in the thicket, then the fire flared up, rosy in the night. Although she could not see him, she knew that the red-haired man was crouching over the fire, his dog beside him. Yesterday she had not known he was in the world, now she belonged to him.

He had been gentle at the last, kissing her, holding her in his arms, making her promise that she would return and that she would tell no one. Tell! As though she would tell. Yes, he had been gentle enough in the twilight, as though offering unspoken apology for his brutality. She remembered his words:

'You belong to me, understand that. To nobody else. And you'll do as I tell you. You'll come back here to-morrow night. No matter how late, I'll be waiting for you.'

And as she had demurred, thinking of the dark river, he had said: 'Yes, you'll come, or I'll come after you. From now on, you'll do as I say.'

And at last she had promised: 'I'll come. Yes, suh, I'll come.'

The day had dragged on to its weary end. Famie had helped Odalie with the household tasks and the ironing for Miss Adelaide. In the afternoon she had scrubbed the floor on hands and knees. Anything to keep from thinking, to make time go by. Her cheeks were flushed and she pressed her palms against her forehead, wondering if it were fever that made her feel so light-headed.

Odalie looked up from her ironing.

'What's the matter, Famie? You act funny today. You sick?'

'No'm, I jus' feel strange.'

The old woman asked: 'Yo' didn' see Numa across the river yesterday, did you?'

Famie's surprise at the question was so convincing

that Odalie said no more. But at supper Bizette brought the boy's name into the talk again.

'Funny, Numa ain't been yeah since Sunday night, an' here 'tis Wednesday. Yo' ain't fuss with him, have yo'?'

The girl shrugged her shoulders and said she didn't know where Numa was, and she didn't care. It was true, she had forgotten him. She thought now of his awkward attempts to caress her, and of how easily she had repulsed him. And as she thought she rubbed her arm where the red-haired man's fingers had bruised her flesh.

It was nearly nine o'clock before Bizette and Odalie went to their room, and it was another hour before their breathing told the girl that they were asleep. She rose then in the dark, bathed and dressed herself. Then she opened the door and went quietly down the steps to the boat.

The moon had not yet risen and the river was black. When she reached midstream, she could see neither bank and she was afraid of losing her way. She raised the oars from the water and listened; there was no sound anywhere except the lapping of the water against the side of the skiff. She rowed a little way and stopped again.

She was lost now in a sea of dark water, suspended in space between black water and blacker sky. Long minutes passed.

At last she heard the clear crowing of a cock. Other cocks answered, and she thought she recognized the note of Bizette's white rooster. She rowed away from the direction of the sound. A few minutes later the bottom of the boat scraped the shore and came to rest. She looked into the darkness, trying to find a familiar landmark. The sky in the east was growing lighter, soon there would be moonlight and she could find her way. She sat in the boat, waiting for the night to lighten.

Not once did she think of turning home again.

When the moon untangled itself from the trees she saw that she had nearly reached her destination; her boat rested on the bank near the Cherokee thicket which she had penetrated yesterday. She pushed off with an oar, and rowed around the point to land that formed the barrier of the inlet. From the shadows a low voice called, 'Who's there?' She went on into the dark.

An unseen hand seized her boat and pulled it ashore. A moment later she was in the man's arms, her fingers in his hair.

The moon hung high above the high-piled clouds. The breeze rippled the river. The man and the girl lay on a blanket spread on the ground under the sycamore tree. She told him how she had lost her way, speaking timidly as though excusing herself for being late for their meeting.

'Why didn't you call?' he asked.

'I didn't know yo' name.'

She could feel the man laughing soundlessly in the dark.

'Call me Joe,' he said. After a pause he spoke again: 'I don't know your name either.'

'Famie.'

'Famie? What kind of a name is that?'

'That's a nickname for Euphémie. I was name' after my mother.'

'French, hanh?'

'Yes, suh.'

'My name's Joe, Famie.'

'Yes, Mister Joe.'

Again she felt his soundless laugh.

'You talk like a little girl. How old are you?'

'I was sixteen jus' befo' Easter, the Tuesday befo' Easter.'

'God, you're nothing but a kid. Just a sweet little kid. You're my little kid, hanh?'

'Yes, suh, if yo' wan' me.'

'You bet I want you. I've got you right here, see? You belong to me now. Every bit of you belongs to me. You understand that?'

'Yes, Mister Joe.'

'Come here, then. Closer.'

'Yes, suh.'

'Kiss me.'

Each night, after the old people were asleep, she crossed the river to meet her lover in the dark thicket. It was the only real thing in her life, for her days were spent in dreams. Odalie thought her ill and insisted on giving her quinine against malaria. Even Bizette, who noticed nothing, thought Famie unusually quiet. She went about the house doing her tasks mechanically. When Odalie was ready to take Miss Adelaide's clothes to the big-house at Yucca, Famie said that she did not want to go; and, shrugging her shoulders, Odalie carried them herself, leaving the girl listless in the doorway.

Alone, she brought the mirror to the light and sat looking at herself. She was glad that she was pretty, and that the man was pleased with her. Often, as they lay in darkness, he would strike a match and hold it near her face, touching her long eyelashes with his fingertip. In the brief light Famie could see his whiteness, his crisp red hair, his steel-blue eyes, contracted against the flame. In the darkness that followed, she would put her hands upon his face, trying to hold his likeness in her fingertips. The nights were increasingly dark now as the moon waned; often she did not see him at all. She might have lain with a stranger and known no difference.

She felt as he told her to feel; she did as she was told to do. And she obeyed his whims blindly. Had he asked her to come away with him, she would have followed without a question.

He told her little enough about himself. He was camping there, alone. He would be there for a long time, perhaps. He had rented the tent and boat from old John Javilée, whose cotton field ended where the thicket on the river bank began. It was Javilée who brought him his supplies and cigarettes once a week. He had seen no one except the old man until Famie came; he did not want to see anyone else now. He was satisfied, he said, to spend his days with the dog, although the dog was not his, either. The setter belonged to Javilée, but had come looking for food, and because he had been fed, he remained.

But he asked Famie many questions about the neighborhood. He was a stranger and it was all natural enough. Once he asked her to bring him a newspaper, and when the girl replied that she never saw one, he laughed. Mr. Guy, over at the commissary, subscribed to newspapers, and the mulatto cotton-planters asked him about the cotton news. But here, in this quiet country, so far from towns and railroads, news of the neighborhood passed from lip to lip. That was all.

He asked, too, about Javilée. Did the old man go about much? Did he mingle with other people? Was he given to gossip? Famie answered no to all these questions, for Javilée was a widower and old, and he lived alone. Famie saw him sometimes at church, but did not know him well, although he was a cousin of Bizette's; but then, all the mulattoes were related. Famie had been about to state the relationship when something the man said stopped the words on her lips:

'What is old man Javilée, anyhow? He looks like he had Indian blood in him. He must be a Cajun, hanh?'

Famie was glad for the darkness that hid her burning face. She realized then that the man did not know she was a mulatto. He thought she was a white girl. She was proud and afraid.

When she did not speak, the man moved near her in the shadow and pulled her close to him:

'I don't know why I'm wasting time talking about that old fool. Come here!'

Numa came to supper on Sunday night, asking Famie if she wanted to go with him to his sister's house. Two men were coming with their guitars and half a dozen young people would be there. They could dance for a while and be back by midnight. She said that she was not well, that she had a headache, and when he insisted, she appealed to Odalie:

'I been ailin' all week, ain't I, *Marraine?*'

Odalie said she didn't know what ailed her as it was too early for malaria. Nevertheless Famie had been taking quinine; she had brought it herself from the store.

'Why don' you ask Nita to go with yo'?' Famie asked. She had spoken innocently, anxious to be rid of Numa, but when she saw the hurt in his face she was sorry. He mistook her smile for coquetry and said at once: 'If yo' don' feel like goin', I'll sit awhile and talk. It won' be no fun without yo', Famie.'

Later, as they sat on the bench under the china tree, he surprised her by saying: 'When yo' goin' to marry me, Famie? Seems like I can hardly wait.'

And when she remained silent, he persisted: 'You love me a little, don' you? There ain't nobody else in the world fo' me.'

In her own happiness she was indifferent to his sincerity. He seemed outside the glow of her affection. When she spoke her words stung him as she never intended them to do.

'Numa, I ain't fo' you. I can't love you like that, like a husban', I mean. Why don' yo' try goin' with some other girl, an' seein' if yo' don' like her better than me?' And as he remained silent, she went on: 'It's the truth, Numa, you've always been like a brother to me, an' I can't think of you no other way.'

He spoke with a passion that surprised and startled her.

'I don' know what's come over you, Famie. You've changed. Not more'n a week ago we sat right here and talked of what we was goin' to do when we got married. *Tante* Odalie knows it. Bizette knows it. It's all fixed. But now somethin's happened, I don' know what. There's some other man, somewhere...'

As she turned to him, startled, he said: 'Is it Christophe Monette? Is he been here, lyin' to yo', tryin' to get you to go off with him to New Awlins? He's bad, Famie. He ain't worth the dirt under yo' foot.'

For a moment the girl was afraid that he had guessed her secret, but when Christophe's name was mentioned, she felt a quick relief.

'Why, yo' mus' be crazy, Numa! I never saw him but once since he got back, and that was at the *fais-do-do*. You were right there the whole time, watchin' every step I took.'

Across the river, in the inlet, the fire sprang into light again, just as it had done a week ago as they sat here together. And again the girl watched it, forgetting the boy beside her. In fancy she saw the man's hair gleaming in the firelight. When the boy beside her spoke again, he took her by surprise.

'Did yo' ever find out who that was, campin' 'cross the river?'

'Yes . . .' She stopped in confusion, then blundered on, 'No, not exactly. It's a white man, I think, but I don't know for sure.'

And as he remained silent, watching her, she went on blindly, 'I don' know who it is, and I don' care. What's it got to do with me?'

She was afraid that he would hear the beating of her heart.

After a time he said: 'I guess I'll be goin' on, Famie.

Looks like everything I say makes yo' mad tonight. I'm sorry. I'll be goin' now.'

She watched him walk down to his rowboat, tied beside hers, watched him fumble with the chain, and push the boat adrift. It was only when he was disappearing in the darkness that she remembered that she had not taken leave of him. She called out:

'Good night, Numa.'

She heard the splash of his oar and listened. He did not answer.

In the darkness the eternal chorus of insects sang the song of summer, and in the black shadow of the tree Famie felt the man's hand tighten on her bare shoulder. She turned her face toward him, her lips against his hair.

'Look, the east is beginning to get light. You must go now, it will be daylight soon.'

'Please, not yet, Mister Joe.' Her mouth was against his throat now: 'What yo' laughin' at?'

'At you.'

'What I do to make you laugh?'

'You called me "mister" again. It's funny.'

'Hol' me close to yo'. Tight. Please.'

'Like this?'

'Yo' hurtin' me.'

'Like this, then?'

'Oh, God knows ... I can't tell you ...'

'Yes, you can. Say it like I taught you to say it. Come on.'

'I love you, Mister Joe ... Now yo' laughin' at me again.'

When he took away his lips, she lay looking out over the water, lighter than the dark shore. Somewhere near-by an owl called and she shivered.

'What's the matter, Famie?'

'That ol' hootin'-owl.'

'Not afraid of an owl, are you? Enough of them around here, God knows ... Is that a tear I feel on your cheek? You're not crying, are you? Just a child afraid of an owl ... Are you really crying? Let's see.'

He fumbled in the dark and a match flared. The tears in her eyes made him seem huge and blurred; only his red hair was vivid in the brief illumination, and the startling whiteness of his skin.

The match went out and lay, a glowing spark on the ground.

She tried to tell him, but she could not. The owl was an omen, and it made her afraid for her happiness. She could only say: 'It's bad luck to hear one cry like that at night.'

'So you cry too, hanh? ... Your tear has a bitter taste.'

Near-by in the thicket came the sharp snapping of a twig.

He threw her from him and sprang away in the darkness. A moment later she saw him crouching, a black shadow against the lighter river, a pistol in his hand.

They both listened, waiting.

After what seemed a long time, he said to her in a whisper:

'Someone was in that bush. There. I heard him. He's gone away now.'

They listened again, but there was no sound except the chorus of insects singing in the grass. He said: 'It might have been an animal of some kind.' Another pause, and then, 'Strange that the dog didn't bark. I wonder where he is?'

# CHAPTER VII

IT WAS a hot day and the clerk in the store was irritable. He had not slept much the night before and he had a headache. He shouted at the mulatto boy who stood on the other side of the counter:

'Goddamit! I've told you no three times and I mean it. Now get on out of here!'

'But I got to have it ...' Numa said.

'Look here, nigger, I'll take a club to you ...'

The boy said stubbornly: 'I'll ask Mr. Guy. He'll lend it to me. He knows me good.'

'The hell he will!'

Numa went out of the store and sat on the edge of the gallery in the sun waiting. Presently the clerk came and stood in the door: 'What do you want with a gun, anyhow?'

'I want to kill a dog,' the boy said; 'I done tol' you that.'

There was a pause while they both looked into the empty road. At last the clerk said: 'What's the matter with you, you sick?'

'No, I ain't sick.'

'Well, you look funny, you breathin' funny,' and as the boy said nothing, the white man said, 'You drunk?'

'No, suh, I ain't drunk.'

'Well, you look drunk or sick or crazy to me. I ain't going to lend no crazy nigger no gun.'

Numa knew that the man was hoping for an opportunity to hit him. The clerk was a hill-man and mean. All hill-men hated negroes, and he knew the clerk hated him more because he was a mulatto and regarded himself as apart from the black field hands. But today's business was too important. There was only one idea in his mind. He must have a gun. He would wait for Mr. Guy; Mr. Guy would lend him one. So he sat there, his feet in the dusty road, waiting.

'You're sweatin',' the clerk said. 'You're sweatin' bad. It ain't all that hot. You must be drunk or sick like I said. You're breathin' funny, too. Breathin' funny an' sweatin' like a horse. Maybe you got a dose an' want to shoot yourself. I guess you got a dose, like all niggers.'

Numa did not answer, looking down the road. Dust was rising in the lane that led from the cotton gin. Two men on horseback were coming. The clerk saw them too.

'If I thought you'd shoot yourself, I might lend you a

gun,' he said. 'But I forgot. Niggers don't kill their-
selves. They ain't got the nerve. So I guess it ain't
that after all.'

Numa shuffled his feet in the dust. He felt as though
he were going to be sick; he had not slept at all last
night and all day he had been wandering in the fields
trying to think. Maybe he did look strange. He tried
to pull himself together so he could ask Mr. Guy to
lend him a gun. No matter what he thought, his mind
went back to that.

The two men rode up to the store gallery. Mr. Guy
was thin and sunburned and wore a panama hat. The
other man was a stranger with a black mustache; there
was a badge on his vest and a revolver in a holster.
Numa had never seen him before. Both men dismounted, tied their horses to the hitching-rack, and
went into the store.

The clerk turned to follow, and said in an undertone
to the mulatto boy: 'That's the sheriff. Why don't you
ask him to lend you his gun?'

Numa sat in the sun, pressing his knuckles to his forehead, waiting. He did not close his eyes, for when he
did he saw always the same maddening picture: a
match flaring in a dark thicket, a girl's bare breasts
and black, tangled hair. He had lived with that picture for many hours now. He must try to behave as he
always did, so when he spoke to Mr. Guy there would
be no difficulty.

The two men were closeted in the office with the door shut, and the clerk was behind the counter pretending to straighten the bolts of calico on the shelf. Numa could hear him moving about. After a long time the sheriff came out, wiping his mustache on a red bandanna handkerchief. Mr. Guy and the clerk stood with him in the door.

'It might be a good idea to tell him to keep a watch out,' said the sheriff, nodding in the clerk's direction, 'although I don't think the man's within a hundred miles of here; he's lit out for New Orleans most likely.'

'Who's that, sheriff?' asked the clerk.

'There's a man wanted by the Texas authorities,' the sheriff said. 'Four fellows held up a bank in San Antonio, killed the teller and another man who was just standing there. There was some shooting and one of the bandits got killed. The other three got away. Two of 'em were caught in Houston, but the third one got over into Louisiana, headed down this way. Personally, I don't think there's a chance of his hiding out around here. Too quiet here; a stranger gets spotted quick, as I was just telling Mr. Randolph. But I thought I'd ride down from town and inquire. The tip came pretty straight, that the man came this way. There's a reward, too. A thousand dollars, but it would be split up about twenty ways, probably, if anybody did land him. But I want to tell you that them Texas cowboys are hard customers. He'll shoot it out, likely as not.

You haven't seen any strangers around, have you? Here in the store, I mean, or passing by?'

'No,' said the clerk. 'Once in a while a strange nigger comes in. I ain't seen a strange white man in God knows when. Not down here. It's like you say, I'll bet he's gone to New Orleans. What does the guy look like, sheriff?'

'Here's his picture. Not a bad-looking bastard, is he? You wouldn't think that a young fellow like that would be wanted for murder, would you?'

'I'll keep a watch out,' said the clerk. 'I'd like to get a chance at that reward.'

'He's not on Yucca, I'm sure of that,' said Mr. Guy. 'I've just made a round of the cabins on the place, and nobody has seen a strange white man in a month.'

'You might go over and ask the priest on Isle Brevelle,' the clerk suggested.

'I've been there, son, but the priest hasn't seen anyone suspicious. Well, Mr. Randolph, I thank you for the drink, and now I'll be on my way back to town.'

Mr. Guy went back to his office and the clerk walked to the edge of the gallery as the sheriff got on his horse again:

'Tell me,' said the clerk, squinting against the sun, 'has the man got any scars or anything to identify him by?'

'Not that I know of,' said the sheriff, 'The description says that identification should be easy, though. He's got fiery red hair.'

The sheriff was well down the road when he saw a thin mulatto boy running after him. He pulled up his horse.

'Wait!' the boy said.

# CHAPTER VIII

FAMIE sat in the doorway gazing out along the furrows; soon it would be sunset, then the friendly dark would come. She counted the hours on her fingers: six, seven, eight, nine, ten o'clock. With good luck she could be in his arms within five hours. Five more hours to wait. She stretched her own slim arms above her head and looked up. Dear God, but she was happy! Her lips moved in prayer, the words of the familiar 'Hail Mary,' and as she repeated them she felt that God's mother was her friend and protector.

Before the doorway the long rows of young cotton plants were green against the red-brown soil, and along the horizon the fluffy clouds were white against the blue. But as she gazed a buzzard passed between her and the sun, a great black bird sailing with outstretched wings. She crossed herself to ward off bad luck as the shadow of

the wings swept the ground at her feet. The bright
bubble of her happiness was gone; she sighed and went
indoors.

Bizette sat sleeping in the back door, a yellow hen
lying in the dust beside his bare feet; behind his sleeping figure the river glittered with its shining ripples and
the thicket beyond the stream lay veiled in a burning
blue haze.

A flock of pigeons flew above the river and the thicket,
whirling by in a smooth circle, returning slowly to the
*pigeonnier* at Yucca. Every afternoon the pigeons circled back and forth across the stream; one could almost
tell the time of day by their flight. Now as they passed
from sight the girl stood watching, waiting for their return.

After a few moments they appeared again, circling
toward the thicket on their second flight. White
feathers caught the sun beneath their breasts as their
bodies tilted against the moving air. Again the feeling
of peace came to the girl as she watched the birds.
How quiet the spring landscape appeared, with each tree
outlined in young green leaves, with the young cotton
pushing up from the new-turned earth, and above in the
golden air the pigeons filling the sky with the stirring
of their feathered wings.

Now the birds were directly above the thicket on the
further shore, and as she watched she saw the flock
hesitate, the lazy circle rudely broken. Abruptly the

flock divided, separated and was gone. And as she wondered, there came the sharp detonation of a gun. The pigeons had heard it first, and had taken flight.

Old Bizette opened his eyes and smiled: 'John Javilée is sho' goin' tuh get in plenty trouble shootin' Mr. Guy's pigeons,' he said. 'Ah tole that ole man to let them pigeons alone.'

It was after ten o'clock before the measured breathing of the two old people assured Famie that they slept. Then she went quickly down the steps to her boat. For hours she had tried to calm her fears, had tried to accept Bizette's explanation for the gunshot which had scattered the pigeons, but her nervousness grew as the hours dragged by; and now, as she fumbled with the knotted rope, she was shaken as though by a chill. Her heart beat painfully as she pushed the skiff away from the steps, and the oars rattled in the oar-locks as she began to row. There was no moon but the stars were bright and she could see her way; there was a soft iridescence on the water and the dark line of the opposite shore could be seen.

When the boat was nearing the entrance of the inlet, she tried to call out, but her voice was only a hoarse whisper; she rowed on into the darkness under the trees and as the boat came to rest among the willows she climbed ashore. The man was not there.

Now she managed to call softly:

'Mister Joe!'

Only stillness, only darkness around her as she awaited his answering call, and then a shadow moved in the brush near-by. She cried out again, this time in wordless terror.

The black-and-white dog emerged from the deep shade and came whining to her feet. For a moment she had a feeling of relief: the dog was here, surely the man must be somewhere near-by. She began to climb the steep path to the clearing where his tent was pitched. In a moment she had reached the top of the bank and the spot where his fire had always burned, but the tent was gone, and the fire had burned itself out. Only a few embers glowed under the ashes.

She swayed, stumbled, and fell to her knees; she felt the warm ashes under her fingers, and felt something else too, something sticky and wet ... She tried to rise, but her knees would not support her, and she fell upon her face in the ashes.

The dog stopped whining, retreated a few steps, raised his head and howled.

It was after three o'clock when Numa found her there, her face in the ashes. He thought at first that she was dead, but when he put his hand upon her shoulder she shuddered. He brought water in his hat and with his handkerchief he bathed her face. She lay with her head against his shoulder while he wiped away the ashes and blood. At intervals he could feel her body quiver.

For more than an hour he held her against him, watching the eastern sky where the horizon was beginning to show gray. His face was gray too and he was near tears.

At last he began to speak to her, telling her that she must let him take her home, that she would be missed, that a search would be made for her. He said the same words over and over and after a long time she seemed to understand him, for she nodded and began trying with shaking hands to put her hair in place. At last she asked a question, her voice so low that he guessed rather than heard the words:

'Is he...?'

She raised her head and looked at him in the early light and his face gave her the answer before she heard the words:

'Yes, Famie, they shot him. He's dead.'

He could not look any longer at her staring eyes, but turned away and covered his face with his hands.

# PART TWO

*NUMA*

# C H A P T E R   I X

THE first thunder of spring wakens the snakes.

Famie kept thinking of that as the lightning flashed in the night. She lay in bed watching the blinding flashes as they came in at the chinks in the shutters and a crack under the door. Blue flickered in the empty fireplace and showed a spider spinning its web between the andirons.

She lay there, smiling to herself, thinking of the snakes in the woods and on the river bank: long black snakes, fat gray snakes, little green snakes, waking up, creeping out from their hiding places, into the rain. She thought of the frogs too, green tree frogs that cry so plaintively as for something lost long ago, fat bullfrogs with their deep hoarse voices, and toads sitting up to their eyes in puddles, enjoying themselves.

Snakes and frogs and the heavy rain. She was afraid

of snakes, but she felt sorry for them, too, for they were always killed on sight. Chicken-snakes stole eggs, and Bizette believed that black snakes sucked cows . . .

And then, as though some forgotten bruise had been hurt again, realization came to her. She had forgotten for a moment that she wanted to die, and with remembrance came tears. She turned her face into the pillow. He was gone, he was never coming back, they had killed him and she was left alone forever.

She had not been able to realize it at first, after that night on the river bank. She was like a woman half awake, she could not remember, she could not believe. She was waiting for the night to come, so that she could go across the river again to find happiness in her lover's arms. Her whole life had centered upon that, and now there was nothing left.

She had been only half conscious when Numa brought her home and put her to bed. But it was her sobbing that awakened Odalie, after Numa had gone and left her there. The old woman, coming in with a lamp, had found her lying fully dressed on the bed. There had been questions, reproaches, demands. But Famie could not answer, she could only cry, and finally Odalie had left her alone in her darkened room. Probably she slept; she couldn't remember. But a day had passed, and a night had gone by. Once when she roused herself, she saw Numa beside her looking at her through the mosquito *baire*, his face dim through the netting . . . He tried to tell her something, to ask her something, but she could only cry and tell him to go away.

But Numa must have talked with Odalie and Bizette, for they asked no more questions. Odalie brought food to her, tried to make her get up and sit in the sun. She was better now, she could talk and work like other people. But tonight, in the storm, she had forgotten for a time that life was over. She had been thinking about snakes and frogs.

The thunder grew louder, the wind shook the house, and old Odalie came into Famie's room with a Holy Candle blessed by the priest. She placed the taper upon the little altar where the Virgin's picture stood, and where a crucifix hung above a vase of wax flowers. Trembling, the old woman knelt before the crucifix, praying for safety from the storm.

Famie pushed aside the *baire* and rose to kneel beside her. And, as the lightning flashed and the thunder roared, the two women knelt there together. Bizette, his 'good' ear in the pillow, slept tranquilly on, his head under the bedclothes, as the rain made a deafening clatter upon the roof and wind screamed in the chimney.

Famie, kneeling in her nightgown, with her black hair in disorder, was staring at the figure of the Christ as though she had seen Him for the first time. The figure there was tortured, dead. His Mother had buried Him with her own hands; she too had lost all that she had loved. Suddenly and for the first time, Famie was conscious of sorrow other than her own. She turned to the old woman: '*Nainaine*, Ah can't stand it. Oh, *Nainaine*, let me die, let me die.'

The old woman took the girl in her arms, 'Po' child,' she said, 'Lemme help yo' back to bed. The lightning ain't as bad as it was ... God done spared us one mo' time.'

After the storm came hot weather. Every day gentle showers watered the fields. The cotton grew tall and green; banana trees unfurled their large translucent leaves in the garden before the door, and the dark polished leaves of the magnolia glittered like metal. There were singing birds in each tree and the air was filled with the droning of bees and the shrilling of locusts. Hot summer, old hot summer had come.

Madame Aubert Rocque was full of gossip when she came late Sunday afternoon to call on her sister Odalie, and she had a long story to tell of the murderer who had been hiding so close to all of them. She was glad he was dead, yes! He might have killed them all. She had heard a hundred details from one of her nephews who accompanied the sheriff and the other white men to the tent in the thicket. The red-haired man had been swimming and was naked when the men came, but he had a gun for all that; it was in his hand when the sheriff fired and the red-haired man had fallen into the fire, riddled with buckshot. The black-and-white setter tried to bite the sheriff — a fool dog, like the old fool who owned him! — but the men had beaten the dog off. John Javilée had been questioned for an hour, and there was even talk of arresting him for harboring a criminal, but the stupidity and simplicity of his answers convinced the sheriff at last, and the men wrapped the dead body in a blanket and took it to town in a wagon. Yes, it had passed Madame Aubert's house and her dogs followed the wagon sniffing death . . . There was a reward, too, but of course the white men would claim that, although someone said that it was a mulatto who told the sheriff of the man's hiding place. Now who could that be? Nobody knew, and the sheriff wouldn't tell. She wished it had been one of her stupid nephews, but no! They had seen the fire on the river bank and had discussed it, but they were too lazy to investigate; they took it for granted that old Javilée lighted a fire there, as it had burned nightly upon his land. What fools young men were! Think how nice it would be to have four or five hundred dollars sewed up in your mattress, or locked up in your *armoire*, or even in the bank in town, yes!

Madame Aubert spoke rapidly in French, and from the adjoining room Famie listened, crouching on the floor, her head against the panels. But when the old woman told of her lover's death, the girl could bear no more. Her teeth chattered, and her head burned, as she raised herself with an effort and tiptoed from the house. The sun blinded her as she staggered toward the bench under the China tree on the river bank.

Until today she had not pictured the details of the death of the red-haired man, she only knew that he was dead; but now, as though borne on the tide of the old women's gossip, other thoughts came, thoughts of half-remembered things. Her mind went back to the night when a twig snapped in the thicket, and to the man's snarling fear. He had said that someone was spying on them, and now she knew that this was true. But who would have come to that remote place at such an hour? Who could have known?

She tried to think clearly, to put events in order. Numa had found her lying half-dead in the ashes. Numa had ... How had Numa known that she was there?

Suddenly her body became rigid, she pressed the back of her hand across her mouth to stifle a scream and sat staring before her with wide, unseeing eyes.

After a long time she saw Odalie and Madame Aubert Rocque leave the house together, their white sunbonnets turning toward each other as they gossiped, their palmetto fans swaying in unison, and their starched calico skirts sweeping the grass on each side of the roadside path. Famie waited until they had passed from sight, then she went down through the furrows to the road.

Two small negro boys were playing with a purple

kite, and she induced one of them to carry a message to Numa, a message that he was to come to her at once. She heard her own voice as though from a distance as she spoke.

'W'at yo' goin' tuh give me, ef'n Ah do dat?' the boy asked, and she replied: 'Ah'll give yo' a piece of cake...'

Why had she said that? She pressed her hands to her forehead trying to think. Cake? Yes, now she remembered. Madame Aubert had brought a piece of cake in a napkin when she came to call that afternoon. Famie had placed it upon the table. Well, the boy could have it.

She turned and went back to the house again. It was sunset and the red glow from the sky came into the room, giving familiar objects an air of unreality. She slumped down at the table and buried her face in her arms.

It seemed a long time before she heard a quick step upon the boards of the porch, and Numa's voice calling her. She raised her head and saw that the light had faded and that the room was full of shadows. Numa stood in the doorway, gasping for breath, and beside him stood the small black boy panting like a dog.

'Famie... Fo' God's sake, what's the matter?... What's...?'

She rose and went toward him.

'Numa, there's somethin' Ah've got to know. You've got to answer me.'

He had never seen her like this before; her hair was disordered and her eyes were wide and black. For a moment he was afraid, as she stood there in the twilight with arm upraised as though to strike him.

But the child, unaware or disdainful of her emotion, pushed between them. 'Wha's my cake?' he asked.

Famie's arm dropped to her side, she turned slowly and looked about her, saw the white napkin and pointed to it. 'There. Take it.'

The child began to remove the cloth, but she cried out sharply: 'Take it! Go away, go away!'

The boy snatched the cake and ran from the door; his bare feet hammered upon the porch, then the sound became faint as he went running through the field.

When it was quite still again, she turned to the man and said: 'Numa, yo' got to tell me the truth. Ah've got to know.'

He stood staring at her, a lock of his dark hair lying across his forehead. But his voice was steady when he spoke.

'What yo' want me to tell yo', Famie?'

'Yo' followed me that night. I know it.' And as he remained silent, she went on: 'I mean the night that you left without telling me good-bye. Yo' followed me in yo' boat.'

He bowed his head and she could no longer see his eyes. 'Yo' spied on me. It was yo' that was hidin' in the thicket.'

He could not answer, for as she spoke the bitterness of that night came back to him again: he saw the flaring of the match in the dark, the white skin and red hair of the man, and the tangled black hair and the round breasts of the girl. He hit his forehead with his hand as though to drive away the thing he saw. He tried to answer, but no words came. He bowed his head, sick for her shame and for his own.

It was only then he realized that she felt no shame, for her voice was proud as she went on: 'An' then, because yo' couldn't have me, yo' hated him, and it was yo' that told the sheriff! It was yo' that killed him! Yo' did it, didn't yo'? ... Answer me! Answer me!'

'No!' Numa heard his own words with surprise. 'No, Ah didn't kill him, Famie!'

He had thought that she would never know. And now, as she accused him, he could not face her hatred. He heard himself repeating: 'No, no.'

'But yo' told the sheriff. It's the same thing. You're just as much a murderer as ef you had killed him yo'self. You're a coward, yo' was afraid to kill him yo'self.'

'Famie ... No. Ah didn't kill him. Ah swear ...'

'What?' She stopped short, leaning against the table. She had wanted to hear him say that it was not true. Numa was her friend, her brother, she had known him always. He couldn't have done that to her.

Seeing his advantage, Numa went on: 'Ah swear ...'

Famie looked up, and in the twilight she could see the

white tortured figure on the crucifix in sharp relief against the dark cross. She rose and took the crucifix from the wall and held it out to him.

'Swear,' she said.

For a second he hesitated, then placed his hand upon the figure of the Christ: 'I swear Ah didn't do it,' he said.

Too late to turn back now. He had lied, and he had sworn to a lie. He had doomed himself forever. His thin shoulders shuddered, but he looked Famie in the eye as he answered:

'Ah love yo', Famie, Ah couldn't lie to yo''; he paused, then went on: 'It's true that Ah followed yo' that night. It's true that Ah saw yo' in the thicket wid' ...' He could not continue, the memory was too cruel. 'But Ah swear Ah never tole the sheriff. Ah didn't have nothin' to do with that.'

Why did he go on talking, lying, damning himself further? He was sure now that she did not believe him. But Famie felt as though a weight had gone from her heart. She had lost her lover, and for a time she thought that she had lost her friend; but Numa would not lie, not to her, not before the crucifix. It was someone else then, someone she didn't know ... Perhaps it was better that way. She would never know now.

She put her arms around Numa's neck, and her body fell limp against his: 'Please excuse me, Numa ... Ah should of known that it couldn't 'a' been yo' ...'

His arms were around her, but he was glad that the twilight hid his face from her. She had come back; she belonged to him again. But why must the misery of this lie drag at his heart? He bent his head and kissed her on the forehead. 'Po' chile,' he said.

And as they stood there, limp in each other's arms, they heard the voices of Bizette and Odalie returning home.

Famie's fingers fumbled for the lamp.

When supper was over, Numa and Famie sat on the bench under the China tree. The moon shone bright on the river and the air was sweet with the scent of mint that grew beside the house.

''Member Easter, Famie?' Numa said. 'Do yo' 'member what Ah asked yo' then?'

It seemed long ago to both of them, yet it had been no more than a month, for the moon was not yet full again.

'Yo' mean...?'

'Won't yo' marry me, Famie,' he said. 'There ain't nobody else in the world fo' me.'

She said: 'Yo' know all about ... everything ... and you still ask me that?'

'Yes, Ah know, an' Ah don' care. Ah wan' yo' an' ef'n yo' don' want me, Ah'm goin' to leave this county. Ah'm goin' far from heah, and Ah'm goin' fo' good.'

She saw the moon distorted through the mist of her

tears, then she bent her head and put out her hand to him.

'Ah can't, Numa...'

'Why can't yo' marry me, Famie?'

'Ah jus' can't, Ah'm...'

'Tell me, please tell me.'

'Ah'm... No, Ah can't say it.'

There was a pause, then he said: 'Ah don't care, Famie. Ah know, an' Ah don' care. Ah'll take care of yo'.'

He could not bring himself to speak of the white man, but he repeated: 'Ah'll take care of yo'. Nobody can say nothin' against yo' name ef yo' and me gets married.'

'Ah know, Numa, an' Ah thank yo' for it. But Numa, Ah jus' can't.'

'Some day, maybe?' he asked.

The girl did not answer.

# CHAPTER X

IN HIS office at the back of the Yucca commissary, Guy Randolph looked up to see Numa standing in the doorway. The white man laid down his pen.

'Come in,' he said. 'You got here in a hurry.'

The mulatto boy took a step into the room and closed the door behind him; the clerk, he knew, was trying to overhear the conversation.

'I've got good news for you, Numa,' Mr. Guy said. 'The trouble about the reward has been straightened out, and I've got something for you.'

'Reward?' It was the thing he feared, something had happened, and now Mr. Guy knew that he had told the sheriff. Mr. Guy would tell, and soon Famie would know.

'You don't mean to tell me that you didn't know that you were entitled to a part of that reward, Numa.

You must have known. Why, if it hadn't been for you, that murderer would have got away. I told the sheriff that I expected a settlement for you; but the reward had to be split up. You're lucky, though; there's three hundred dollars for you. I've got it here in the safe.'

'But the sheriff promised that he wouldn't tell...' Numa said.

'Yes, I know,' Mr. Guy said. 'He told me that he promised to keep still about it, although I don't see why. You're due credit, it seems to me, for helping the law.'

The white man opened the safe and took out an envelope from which he extracted a roll of bills. Numa had never seen a twenty-dollar bill before, and as Mr. Guy spread them out on the desk the boy's eyes widened. There were fifteen bills in the envelope, and Mr. Guy counted them out.

'Sign here,' he said, offering a pen to Numa. 'This is the receipt that goes back to the Texas authorities. I've already signed for you, as far as the sheriff here is concerned, but I've got to furnish proof that I've turned over the money.'

'No, suh,' Numa said. 'Ah'm sorry, Mister Guy, and Ah thank yo' fo' it, but Ah don' want it.'

'Don't want...?' Mr. Guy was irritated. 'After all the trouble that I took to get it for you, you stand there and tell me that you don't want it. Are you crazy?'

'No, suh. Ah thank yo' suh, but Ah can't.'

'Why, for God's sake?'

'It's blood money.'

The white man controlled his anger and said: 'Sit down, Numa, and let me talk to you.'

The boy sat on the edge of one of the straight chairs, and Mr. Guy went back to his desk. The money lay between them on the green blotting paper.

'Now see here,' the planter said. 'It's like this, Numa. That man was a murderer, and he was hiding here. There was a reward for his capture, dead or alive. I think I see what you mean when you say it's blood money; you told the sheriff where he was, and the sheriff had to kill him to catch him. But the sheriff killed in self-defense. It was no more than killing a mad dog.'

A mad dog. The phrase made Numa wince, for these were the very words he had used on the day when he tried to borrow a gun from the clerk. He could not explain this to Mr. Guy; he could only say: 'Ah feel like there's blood on that money. Ah don' want it.'

'Stop being a fool, Numa,' said Mr. Guy, 'and listen to me. I've known your father and your grandfather before you. They were both good old men. They were honest, and they knew me when I was a boy. I feel that I know better than you do about this. It was because I knew your family that I insisted that you get what was rightfully yours. I wouldn't see you cheated out of it just because you're not a white man. Now I want you to take this money and put it in the bank. Later, you'll thank me for this. It will be a nest egg for you. You'll be getting married and you'll need it.'

'Will anybody know about it?' the boy asked.

'No,' Mr. Guy said. 'Although I swear I can't see...' And then as an idea occurred to him: 'You're not afraid that some of the white man's friends will come and kill you, are you? You haven't seen any suspicious-looking strangers around here, have you?'

'No, suh... It's somethin' else. Ah don' want *nobody* to know.'

Mr. Guy shrugged his shoulders. Negroes were hard enough to understand, but mulattoes were worse.

'Here, sign this,' he said. 'There at the bottom of the page where the cross is.'

Numa began tracing his signature awkwardly. It took a long time for him to put his name there, and it looked strange to him as he saw it: Numa Lacour.

Mr. Guy was sorry that he had taken the trouble to stand up for the mulatto's rights. Numa stood holding the bills in his hand.

'An' nobody won't ever know?' he repeated.

'Not unless you tell 'em,' said the white man, and turned back to his desk again.

Numa went away. As he passed out through the store the clerk said in a low voice: 'Well, nigger, did you ever get that gun you was looking for that day?'

Numa bit his lip and did not reply.

There was an old wooden clock on the mantel at home, a clock that had belonged to his grandfather, and it was here that the boy hid the fifteen bills. He spread them out flat in the bottom of the clock-case beneath the pendulum, then he cut the top of a cigar box until it fitted snugly above them. The wood looked new, so he smeared it with oil and ashes, then wiped it dry. The money was safe there, and it could stay hidden forever, and nobody would ever know.

And yet, the clock seemed different somehow. Its quiet tick-tock never sounded insistent before, but now he heard it as he lay in bed unable to sleep. Its measured ticking was in unison with his slow-beating heart. He tried to put the thought of the afternoon from his mind, but he found that he could not. From the next room came the measured breathing of his mother; he wished that she were awake so that he could talk to her. His head burned and his thoughts would not let him rest. A month ago he had been happy, a boy in love; but now he was a guilty man. Why, why had this thing happened to him? His only fault had been that he loved Famie, and she had betrayed him. He should hate her for that, but he could not. And yet, in this short space between full moon and full moon, he had killed a man, yes, killed him as surely as though he fired the shot himself. That was his jealousy, but it was cowardice that made him swear that he had no part in the man's murder; and now he had taken the blood money because he was afraid to refuse.

He sat on the edge of his bed, his face in his hands. He must go away. His old uncle lived in Opelousas, nearly a hundred miles from Cane River. Perhaps, Numa felt, he could forget his misery if he went there.

'Ah'm goin' to leave this country,' he said aloud. 'Tomorrow Ah'm goin'. Ah'm never comin' back.'

But he knew that he must return; he knew that some day he must see Famie again. Some day she would turn to him. Some day...

The old clock whirred, its tired spring creaked, and through the darkness came three muffled strokes.

Numa beat his fists against his forehead. 'Oh, time, pass quick. Oh, daylight, come soon. Let me go. Let me go.'

# CHAPTER XI

THE sounds of summer flowed by on the tranquil air. There were distant cries from the cotton gin, and the reverberation of heavy machinery; the whistle sounded, sharp and clear, then a change in the engine's hum as the cotton bale was compressed. Another bale was begun and the engine resumed its even vibration.

In the lanes the cotton wagons waited their turn at the gin, and white fragments of cotton bordered the dusty road where the wagons had passed ... August.

Then warm September rain dripped from the eaves and yellow flowers bloomed along the ditches; the first yellow leaves appeared on the China trees, the first breath of autumn came with the early mornings; there was a feeling of death and decay in the midst of the lingering heat.

The pecans hung in their green husks on the trees,

gathering oily nutriment, hanging there, waiting for the first frosts to detach them and let them fall upon the sodden soil, for now, after the long dry days of July and August, September's soothing rain fell into the parched furrows, going deep into the waiting soil.

Famie stood in the doorway, supporting her swollen body against the door-frame. She felt the child stir.

Numa had been gone for more than five months. She thought of him now, as she looked out into the empty field where water stood between the cotton rows.

There had been so little she could say to him as he stood in the sunlight telling her good-bye. She remembered it all so well: his threadbare coat, his haunted eyes. One word from her, she knew, would keep him there, but she could not say that word. Now she almost wished that she had spoken, for today she felt friendless and desolate indeed.

Yet she was glad that Numa could not see her, for she felt that she was ugly and awkward: she did not want anyone to see her. Her grandmother, fortunately, concurred in this. She agreed that Famie should keep her secret as long as possible. It was, said Odalie, a bad business, but it was Famie's own affair.

What the old woman knew Famie could not guess, but Odalie and her sister, Madame Aubert Rocque, had discussed the matter many times. Everything was arranged for the child's birth, and Lizzie Balize, the negro midwife, had been engaged for mid-December.

Summer had passed like a fevered dream, and little by little Famie became reconciled to her lover's death. At first she would wake, crying out in the night; but now she slept dreamlessly as she used to do. Small things occupied her days, and she helped Odalie with the ironing as she had always done. There was a difference, though, for now Famie examined each article belonging to Mrs. Randolph's baby with intent eyes. Her child should have clothes like these, she decided; her child should have such clothes as white children wear.

Buying the cloth to make the clothes was another matter, for there was no money. Bizette had no luck with his cotton this year, and after his yearly account was settled at Mr. Guy's commissary there was little left. A few necessary articles were purchased, but nothing else. Old Odalie was firm in her decision that every penny must be saved. 'I've known a woman to die fo' lack of five dolla's,' she said, and Famie knew that it was true enough.

The girl's dark eyes clouded as she thought. Lizzie Balize was a good nurse, but suppose...? There was not enough money, Famie knew, to get a doctor.

The girl sighed and turned away from the door. From the *armoire* she took a work basket and brought it to the table. There was a small blanket which she had cut from a large one, avoiding the worn-out places; it was soft from many washings, and the girl had hemmed it with pink worsted. There were some simple clothes, too, made from cotton and trimmed with lace ripped from an old dress. The things were poor enough, as she thought of the fine linen which she washed and ironed each week for Mr. Guy's wife; but even these simple garments would suffice. Later on, maybe, she could do better. Perhaps Miss Adelaide would give her some out-grown dresses. Famie sat listlessly, a faint smile on her face; surely Miss Adelaide would give her something for the baby, but the girl knew that she must wait; she was ashamed for the white woman to see her now.

One day was like another: there was always the quiet river, and the brown fields stretching away. The bare cotton stalks had been plowed under and the fields lay waiting for another spring. The trees were losing their leaves, and she could see houses now that were invisible in the summer time; through the clear autumn air she watched the blue smoke rise from the chimneys at morning and evening, and she knew that women were crouching before the hearths cooking for their men.

In December the evening sky was red along the horizon and the blue mists hung in the trees and softened the sharp outline of the white church across the river; the church and the bare trees and the red sky reflected themselves in the water and made her think of a Christmas card that Sister Désirée had shown her long ago.

Famie was thinking of that picture as she crouched before the fireplace early in the morning of the day before Christmas. The coffee was dripping and the pleasant aroma filled the room. Suddenly she paused with her hand pressed against her body. She was afraid. Her sharp cry aroused Odalie and the old woman came in, tripping over her long flannel nightgown.

The coffee was forgotten as Famie was put back into the bed she had left only a few moments ago; she was surprised to feel that the covers were still warm from her body. It was not long before the pain stopped, but her breath came fast and her eyes were wide as she lay waiting for the agony to come back again.

Odalie finished dripping the coffee, dressed herself, and sent Bizette hobbling through the furrows to fetch Madame Aubert Rocque and the negro midwife, Lizzie Balize.

# CHAPTER XII

IT WAS twilight on Christmas Eve when Numa rode down the muddy lane toward the yellow lamplight which shone from the window of his mother's house. There was the smell of wood smoke and sizzling bacon in the frosty air. His old white horse whinnied as Numa opened the gate, and from the barn came an answering nicker from the roan mare. The boy felt his breath quicken at the familiar sight and sound and smell of home.

His mother — how old she seemed! — cried out in glad surprise when he opened the door. He held her in his arms and realized how cruel he had been to leave her alone so long; but he could not speak of it, and instead he pretended interest in the white cat which lay purring beside the fire, four spotted kittens nursing at her breast. The yellow puppy had grown into a large dog,

and he came sniffing at Numa's trousers, only half
recognizing him, wagging his curly tail doubtfully as
though not quite sure whether he would be patted or
kicked. Numa took the dog's head between his hands
and looked into the animal's pale blue eyes.

He smiled at his mother. 'He sho' grew up to be a
nigger dog.'

The old woman laughed. 'He's good though,' she
said. 'He was plenty company fo' me while yo' was
gone.'

At supper they were very polite to each other, talking
with constraint as though they were strangers, asking
each other questions, answering nicely. Numa told her
how long the ride seemed: it had taken him three full
days, the roads were so muddy, and the distance so
great. He had only been able to make about thirty
miles a day. But he had brought a present with him.
Tomorrow he would give it to her.

The talk of Christmas worried his mother; she apolo-
gized that she had made no preparations for his return.
How could she? She had not known that he was coming. But there was a fine piece of pork in the smoke-
house, and she would bake a cake for him.

Supper was scarcely over when there came a call
from outside and old Madame Lacour cried out in astonishment. How could she have forgotten! She had
promised to go to midnight Mass with her brother and
his wife. They were going early in a wagon, and they

had come for her. They expected to make a round of visits on the way, stopping at the homes of friends, gathering their kinfolks until the wagon was full, and then going over on the flatboat to the midnight services. In the excitement of Numa's arrival she had forgotten all about it; she was not dressed. Never mind, she would go and tell them that she could not go.

But Numa interrupted her. Surely she must go; he was too tired to take her; he wanted to go at once to bed. He went outside to tell his uncle and aunt to wait while his mother dressed.

They were pleased to see him, crying out in high voices. He climbed up into the wagon. They kissed him on both cheeks, and said how glad they were that he had come home. Old Amédée Lacour liked Numa and thought it a shame that he had left his mother alone for so long a time. His wife, looking like a shapeless bundle under her coat and knitted shawl, said shrilly that the girls at the last *fais-do-do* had asked her why Numa had run away. It was high time that he came home again. He should join them that night, fatigue or no fatigue, for there would be many pretty girls at Mass. Aie-yie!

She cackled with laughter.

Before long Numa's mother emerged, bundled up in coat and shawl, and Numa helped her climb over the wheel and into one of the chairs which stood in the wagon bed; she carried a blanket because she was sure that she would be cold crossing the river. Finally everything was arranged, and the boy watched the wagon go creaking down the lane and splashing through the puddles.

As he re-entered the house the old clock whirred and struck eight. Numa started guiltily. Through its glass door he could see the bottom of the clock-case, and he saw that the greasy dust lay undisturbed as he had left it.

'Nobody knows,' he said aloud.

But even as he spoke there came a quick rapping behind him, and the boy turned sharply toward the uncurtained window. But it was only the yellow cur, who at the sound of Numa's voice was beating his tail on the floor.


Numa's boots sloshed through the puddles.

He told his mother that he was too tired to accompany her, and yet, the minute her back was turned, he put on his heavy boots and went out. He smiled in the darkness as he hurried.

Despite all his resolutions, he felt that he must see Famie at once. He had a present for her, and now he carried it carefully in his hand. In a store window in Opelousas he had seen it, and he had bought it for her, spending nearly his last dime in order to buy it. The thing that he carried so carefully was a small bisque statue of a bride and groom such as are sometimes used

on wedding cakes. He knew that she would smile when
she saw it. Perhaps she would be ready to marry him
now. It seemed years since he had seen her, and no
letters had passed between them.

As he left the lane and entered the path between the
furrows which led to old Bizette's house, he felt so light-
hearted that he could have laughed aloud. He pictured
the family gathered at the hearth, and he thought of
Famie's surprise when he entered with his Christmas
present in his hand. As he opened the gate from the
lane he heard negroes shouting in the fields and the
sound of popping firecrackers from the direction of the
commissary. The folks at Yucca, white and black, always set off fireworks at Christmas time.

But as he approached the house he saw at once that
something was wrong. There were two horses tied to
the posts of the porch, and a man sat huddled on the
steps. Inside the house there were running steps, and
the windows were bright behind tightly closed curtains.

And as he approached he heard a woman scream. It
was unlike anything he had ever heard before, a thin,
long-drawn-out shriek of agony. The man on the steps
raised his head as Numa came close; it was Bull Balize,
the black son of Lizzie the nurse.

'Dey tole me not to let nobody in, not *nobody*,' the
negro said. 'She's havin' a ha'd time.'

And then, in response to Numa's quick questions,
Bull told him that Famie Vidal had been in agony all

day. Old Bizette sent for Lizzie Balize shortly after sun-up, and Lizzie had come at once. But something was wrong. Lizzie had tried every remedy she knew, even to putting an axe under the bed to cut the pain, and the old women had assisted her. But Famie still screamed. It made Bull sickish just to listen to it, he said.

Still uncomprehending, Numa asked: 'What's the matter with her?'

'Ah don' know what a-matter wid 'er, cep'n she's havin' a mighty ha'd time havin' dat baby,' the negro said.

Numa felt as though someone had slapped him across the mouth. The small figure of the bride and groom slipped from their wrappings of tissue paper and lay in the mud beside his boot.

Madame Aubert Rocque and Odalie said that Numa saved Famie's life. They thought the girl would surely die, and even black Lizzie was scared, yes! although she would not admit it. When things were at their worst, Numa had brought the doctor.

That Numa! When he heard that Famie was so sick he had ridden ten miles to Cloutierville and had shown the white doctor a twenty-dollar bill. That brought him, yes, sir! The boy and the white man had driven over the dark, muddy, and dangerous roads and they arrived together at sun-up on Christmas morning.

Famie was exhausted, but the doctor knew things which were beyond the skill of the midwife. The baby was born and the girl was sleeping within an hour after his arrival. It was all over... Numa brought a quart of fine whiskey, too, and the old women cried 'Noël!' as the white man drank before leaving.

The old women talked to each other, to Numa, to Lizzie, to anyone who would listen. They said the same things over and over, adding details, laughing in relief, as they sat sipping hot toddies beside the hearth. There is a time when whiskey is good, yes, when women are tired... That Numa! He thought of everything. At last they went to sleep, each in her chair beside the fire. In the four-post bed Famie slept too, worn out with agony, and the child slept beside her.

Lizzie busied herself setting the house to rights, looking scornfully around her. Humph! These mulattoes were as uppity as white people, making all this fuss about a baby. And that Numa was a plum fool, bringing the doctor there and acting as though Lizzie did not know her business. Well, he wouldn't be so pleased when he saw the baby, for the child was surely not his.

'Yessuh,' she said aloud, 'ef'n dat chile's paw ain't a white man, my name ain't Lizzie Balize.'

# CHAPTER XIII

CHRISTMAS was gay at Yucca Plantation that year.
Early in the morning Mr. Guy opened a keg of whiskey
on the gallery before the commissary and gave liquor to
all the negro men on the place. It was an old custom
held over from slave times: his father and his grandfather had done so before him. By eight o'clock many
of the negroes were reeling and rocking as they went
home through the muddy cotton rows, and some of
them had fallen into fence corners and lay snoring until
they were hauled home by their staggering friends or by
their women.

Those who imbibed more moderately tried shooting
at the *papegai* — another Christmas custom.

A cow had been butchered and divided into the usual
cuts, and the beef lay arranged in order on a large
wooden table. The beef was all given away to the ten-

ants and laborers; the choice cuts were prizes for marksmanship.

The *papegai* was a crude wooden cow cut from boards and was painted red and yellow; this effigy was placed high on a pole, and the negro men took turns shooting at it with a rifle from a line forty yards away. The oldest had first shot; the younger men waited, and the boys came last of all. The men aimed at the part of the animal which they considered the best cut and which they desired most as food. They stood in line and awaited their turns, whooping applause for those whose aim was accurate, and jeering at the unsuccessful marksmen.

'Look at Papa Chawlie. He goin' tuh bust dat rump-roast!'

'Betcha he ain't!'

'Whoo-oo!'

Ping! The rifle sounded sharp on the frosty air, and there was a shout as the old man's bullet struck the *papegai* on the head instead of the tail.

'De ole man's got tuh eat brains!'

'Maybe he wants de tongue!'

Whiskey had done its work, and some of the men missed the target altogether. But in time each one hit some part of the effigy and the beef was distributed accordingly.

'There's one thing to be said for a cow,' said Mr. Guy, laughing as two men disputed a coveted portion. 'There are two pieces of nearly everything.'

Negro women, wearing blue or red dresses and checkered head-handkerchiefs, cheered for their men, and
children screamed with excitement as they set off firecrackers: for fireworks — so prized by all children —
were a part of the celebration at Yucca. Each child
received a pack of firecrackers, and this year each one
got two Roman candles to boot. The latter were saved
for night.

The negroes were merry in the muddy road beside the
river: dogs barked, and horses tied to the fences reared
and showed the whites of their eyes when firecrackers
exploded near them. The rifle and firecrackers popped
almost continuously, and the smell of gunpowder hung
in the air.

At last it was over, and the men and women went
homeward, the children trailing after them, and the
curs following behind. The red and blue and yellow
clothes were vivid against brown earth and dark
trees.

Mr. Guy, watching them from the gallery of the commissary, saw smoke begin to rise from the chimneys of
the nearer cabins, and he knew that Christmas dinners
were in preparation.

All this was a party for the negroes: the mulattoes
took no part in it. There were many mulatto men and
boys in the crowd, spectators who had come to see the
fun. The old men, wearing wide black felt hats above

their clear-cut faces, stood together recalling the time when *Grandpère* Augustin had similar parties for his slaves in the days before the Civil War.

When the negroes had all gone, Mr. Guy invited five of the old mulatto men inside the commissary and took them back into his office. There, beside the stove, he opened a bottle of fine whiskey, and filled six small glasses. It was a yearly custom. Mr. Guy recognized the difference between negroes and mulattoes; it was this little social distinction that made the mulattoes like him. Not one of them would have drunk with the negroes, nor did they expect or even desire Mr. Guy to drink publicly with any mulatto; but this little private ceremony on Christmas was a custom of long duration. It established something. Mr. Guy was a gentleman and understood things.

The clerk, who was not invited to drink, stood by eyeing the group critically. He disapproved of the whole business, and he thought that Mr. Guy spoiled the mulattoes: 'Just a damned race of bastards,' he said to himself. It irritated him, too, that Mr. Guy felt himself so superior that he could afford to drink with a race other than his own. Back in the hills where *he* came from such things were unheard of. Men had been tarred and feathered for such carryings on. At that moment he hated Mr. Guy and his superior ways, and he hated Miss Adelaide, who never invited him into the parlor when company came. He was just a servant, like the niggers, in spite of the fact that he ate at the table with the white people.

He couldn't understand these distinctions. There were really four classes on Cane River: Mr. Guy and his kind, and then his, the clerk's kind — he knew that Miss Adelaide considered him 'trash' — then there were the mulattoes who looked down upon the black people, and last, at the bottom of the heap, were the negroes themselves ... And the negroes didn't seem to give a single damn!

'They're all damned niggers to me,' he said to himself.

But as he stood watching the old men drinking with Mr. Guy, an unwelcome thought came to him: Nita looked white, but she was a nigger too. Well, what difference did it make? All women, white, yellow, or brown, were for man's pleasure. Men had to take what they could get.

Yet some of his friends, back in the hills, would call him a 'nigger-lover' if they knew. The clerk felt his face flush at the thought, but he brushed the idea aside: 'Jus' let 'em try it, that's all,' he thought. 'Besides, nobody knows nothin' about it, and they won't, neither.'

The old men finished drinking, and put on their hats again. Then they all shook hands with Mr. Guy and wished him luck for the new year.

'Good-bye, Mister Guy.'

'Good-bye, Henri.'

'Good luck, Mister Ran'off.'
'Good luck, Ulysse.'
'Good-bye, Mister Guy.'
'So long, Telesmon.'
'*Au revoir, Monsieur Guy.*'
'*Au revoir, Narcisse.*'
'Happy New Year, Mister Guy.'
'The same to you, Bizette.'

# CHAPTER XIV

NUMA slept nearly all day.

His mother had prepared a dinner which she knew he liked: pork roast, sweet potatoes, and collards, and she had baked a cake; but when she looked into his darkened room and saw him lying in the deep sleep of exhaustion, she sighed and went away without waking him. Hey law! All her preparations were for nothing. Nevertheless, Numa was a good boy, and she was so glad he had come back to her that nothing else mattered. So she put the meat and vegetables on the back of the stove to keep them warm, and set the cake away in a cupboard. She would wait and eat with him when he woke up.

In the afternoon she busied herself with the usual outdoor tasks: she fed the horses and the chickens, and milked the cow. The white cat came out of the house into the slanting sunshine and rubbed against the old woman's skirts. She poured milk into a blue bowl and talked to the cat as the animal satisfied its hunger. They were together so much that she almost believed that the cat understood what she said, and like so many lonely people, she frequently spoke aloud, addressing animals or even inanimate objects.

'*Minou*, Ah sho' ought to get rid o' yo',' she said. 'Eve'body knows a white cat brings bad luck. Jus' havin' yo' in the house makes me a po' woman. Some of these days, Ah'm goin' to run yo' off and get me a yellow *minou*. That'll bring gold to me sho'. Yes, ma'am, Ah'm goin' to run yo' off from heah.'

She petted the animal as she spoke and her voice was caressing. The white cat arched her back and purred.

Numa stirred from sleep and stretched his tired body. He was stiff and sore. The ride through the night had been nearly too much for him, tired as he was from the long trip home. His head was hot and his hands were cold, and he felt as ill in mind as he did in body. Nevertheless he threw back the covers, rose, and went to the fireplace. The embers still smouldered, so he added some light wood and a handful of dried moss and the fire flickered up.

His mud-spattered clothes hung on a chair, and he picked up his trousers and felt in the pockets: there was a roll of bills, and he spread them out and counted them.

Last night when he ran home and pried the false bottom from the clock-case, the money had been as he left it, but now forty dollars was gone. Twenty for the doctor, and two for the whiskey, and eighteen in his pocket. Fortunately in the excitement, nobody had questioned him as to his possession of so much money; they had taken it for granted that he had earned it in his absence. Well, he would keep the eighteen dollars and use it as he pleased. But the rest of the reward must remain hidden, for if he spent it people would surely guess his secret. He pressed the false bottom back into place, hiding the money from sight. Two hundred and sixty dollars remained there.

As he put the eighteen dollars back into his pocket, his exploring hand brought out the small bisque figures of the bride and groom. They were smudged with mud, but were otherwise uninjured. The boy's mouth twisted as he looked at them. But a moment later he had poured water into the bowl on the washstand and was cleaning the ornaments carefully. Well, why not? What did it matter?

How quiet the house was. His mother must be outdoors. The small bride and groom made him smile. He would go tonight and give them to Famie, just as he had intended to do.

When he had finished washing and dressing himself, he went to the window and pushed open the shutters. His mother sat on a block of wood not far away; she was stroking the white cat as it lapped milk from a blue dish. At the sound of the creaking shutter she rose and re-entered the house.

'Son?' she called.

Numa went into the kitchen and kissed her. She asked no questions as to his absence overnight, but smiled as she began to set the dinner on the table. Numa was grateful to her. Everything was going to be all right.

When they had finished and were sitting with the coffee-cups beside the fire, he gave her the present which he had brought home from Opelousas: enough cotton material for a dress. She fingered the cloth and said how pleased she was; it was exactly what she wanted, and unlike the cloth in the commissary at Yucca. Her pleasure was so genuine that he felt a warm glow of affection for her.

'An' that ain't all,' he said.

She looked at him expectantly: 'What yo' mean, son?'

He reached into his pocket and brought out the small roll of bills and counted out ten dollars: 'Look,' he said, and put the money into her hand.

Numa saw his mother's face change as she sat with the money lying on her lap. For a moment he was afraid that she was going to ask a question, but she did not. At last she said:

'Yo're good to me, Numa, and Ah thank yo' fo' it, but yo' need it yo'seff. Ah'm ole, an' Ah've got eve'-thing Ah need. Yo' keep it, son, an buy yo'seff a suit o' clothes. Yo' lookin' plum ragged.'

'Ah'll make out all right,' Numa said. 'Ah don' wan' no new suit now. Soon it'll be spring, and Ah'll be plowin'.'

A bar of late sunlight shone through the window into the ashes of the fireplace and dimmed the pale flames which burned along the lower side of the smouldering logs. The sunlight fell upon the yellow cur sleeping between them on the hearth, and the dog whined in his sleep and his four paws quivered as though he were running.

'He's chasin' dream rabbits,' the old woman said.

The boy sat thinking, wondering. Why was it so hard to speak? Why are the simplest things the hardest to say? His mother was trying to say something to him and he dreaded to hear it, yet he did not for a moment doubt her loyalty and affection. What did she know? What did she guess? He looked at her, but she sat gazing into the fire as though fascinated by the sunlight upon flame and ashes.

At last she spoke and as her meaning became clear to him, he started with surprise.

'Numa, yo' is a man now, an' yo' ought to be thinkin' 'bout gettin' married. It ain't natu'al fo' a man to stay by himse'f.'

She saw the haunted look in his eyes, and put out her hand to him. 'Ah know all 'bout it, son,' she said.

He felt the blood rushing to his face, but he forced himself to say: 'Know about what?'

'About yo' an' Famie Vidal.'

'But Famie...' He could not go on, but sat staring at his mother. Her eyes were wet and two tears ran down her cheeks; she made no effort to wipe them away.

'Odalie tol' me right after yo' went away.'

'Odalie tol'...?'

No, she could not go on talking that way. She could not say the words. She tried in another way to tell him.

'Numa, son... Ah know Famie is fo' yo'... Ah mean, Ah know there ain't no other woman that yo' cares about. Odalie knows it too. Odalie and Madame Aubert an' me, we talk plenty about it.' A pause, and then: 'Ah talk with Odalie this mornin'.'

Numa's hands were clenched as he waited for her to go on. He could not meet her eyes.

'It ain't Famie's fault, son, not all of it. Famie's good. She ain't a bad one like Nita. Ah've watch' Famie growin' up...'

No, that was not right either. The old woman tried another way.

'It ain't the firs' time somethin' like that happened on Cane River, an' it won' be the las'.'

That was all, she could say no more.

Famie lay in the big four-post bed, her dark hair spread out on the high-piled pillows, the child nursing at her breast. A red card, stuck against the lamp chimney, reflected a rosy glow upon her. In the soft light her skin was gold colored, and her eyes were large and black. To Numa, who sat in a chair beside the bed, she had never been so beautiful. Odalie had gone into the other room, leaving them together.

It was New Year's Eve, and they could hear the far-away shouts of negroes in the fields, but in the room it was quiet. The fire flickered on the hearth and the kettle on its trivet sent forth a thin plume of steam. Everything seemed warm and safe.

Beyond greeting each other they had said nothing, although she had turned back the covers so that he could see the baby, a strong, healthy boy with blue eyes. His hair was like fine down, but there was no mistaking its color; it was red.

But, someway, Numa did not care any longer about the red-haired man. He was gone and Famie was his own again. Although no words had passed between them tonight, he knew that she had turned toward him; she had taken him back.

From his pocket, he took the toy figures of the bride and groom and placed them upon the sheet. She touched them with a fingertip and smiled.

'Fo' me?' she asked. He nodded.

She understood what he meant, and put her fingers upon his lips.

A week after Easter Famie and Numa were married.

The young cotton was green in the fields and the catalpa and locust trees were blooming in the lanes. The air was sweet and warm and the sun shone bright as Odalie, Famie, and Bizette crossed the river in a skiff; and as they climbed the steep path from the river to the priest's house the air was filled with the sleepy song of bees.

A small group had gathered in the checkered shade of the trees beside the church on Isle Brevelle. Numa's mother came to greet them, very fine in her freshly laundered black and white print dress; Madame Aubert Rocque wore lavender-flowered cotton, pale from many washings, and Nita, strangely subdued today, looked almost like a nun in her plain gray frock. She stood looking curiously at Famie as the girl came through the sunlight into the shade, her white ruffles brushing the grass.

It was the same white dress that she had worn on Easter a year ago, but now there were faint rust stains on the skirt, stains which no washing could remove and which had come from the chain of her rowboat on those dark nights when she had crossed the river to meet her lover in the thicket. But that was all behind her now; it seemed a long time past ... Because she was a bride today, Famie had removed the red flowers from her hat and had substituted a twist of white ribbon. She smiled shyly as she greeted those who waited in the shade by the cemetery wall.

The old men stood in one group, and the old women in another; the boys and girls came forward to meet her, smiling, their hands outstretched. She felt the girls' kisses on her cheeks, and smelled the *vertivert* which they used as perfume. Then the boys were shaking her hand, and Numa was holding her arm. Madame Aubert Rocque had a present for her, an old ivory-bound prayer book, now yellow with age.

Everyone there was related to her; each was her aunt, her uncle, or her cousin. Numa and Famie were related too, for that matter, but the priest had secured a dispensation from his religious superior in town in order that second cousins might be married. For three Sundays the banns had been read out in church, and now all that remained was the ceremony and the signing of the register.

When the plantation bell at Yucca rang for noon the group moved towards the priest's house. Father Broussard received them in his study and the room seemed dim and cool after the sunlit churchyard. It was so still in the room that, when he paused, she could hear the trilling of a wren in the cemetery near-by. She felt the cool ring slip upon her finger, and heard the priest's words as though they came from some far-off place. She felt as though she were dreaming.

The priest stopped talking and shook her hand,

Numa kissed her, and she turned to see the old women standing in a row against the wall, smiling at her above their swaying palmetto fans.

It was all over.

The newly married pair went home together in the skiff, while the others walked in single file along the narrow path toward the spot where the flatboat lay moored. As Numa rowed out into the placid blue of the river, he smiled, and Famie, turning in her seat, looked back over her shoulder. Outlined against the sky at the top of the incline the group spread out like a procession, and as she looked they waved to her: the old men raised their black hats, and the women waved their fans. The girl in the boat raised her arm in answer to their salute. It was only at this moment that the thought came to her: 'This is the end of something: after this everything will be different.'

Numa tied up the boat, and together they climbed the eleven steps which led to the door. The house was still, the doors stood open, but the green window shutters were half-closed against the heat of the day. As they crossed the threshold, Numa put his arms around her and pressed his body against hers. She gave him her lips and put her arms around his neck.

'Ah, Famie...' he said. 'Ah've waited an' waited.'

But as he spoke the shrill sound of a crying child came to them. Famie turned in his arms and looked about her. Again came the cry and she left him and ran through the house and out of the front door. Lizzie Balize sat in a chair in the shade of a tree by the well, the baby in her lap.

'They ain't nothin' the matter wid 'im,' said Lizzie, as the girl took the baby into her arms. 'He's been sleepin' evah since yo' went away, an' now, jes' as soon as yo' gits back, he start squallin'! He's jus' hongry, dat's all.'

There was a swirl of skirts as the girl took the chair that the black woman had just quitted, and with a quick gesture she unfastened the back of her dress, pulled it down over one shoulder, and offered her breast to the child. Dancing spots of sunlight came through the pale green leaves and fell upon her white hat and dress and upon the gold-colored flesh of her shoulders and breast. A bright beam of light fell upon the child's clutching fingers and red hair.

In the doorway Numa stood forgotten. His shoulders sagged and his eyes were sad as he looked at the figures beneath the tree beside the well, for at that moment he realized that, in Famie's affections, the white man's child would always come first.

That night the young people of the neighborhood came to serenade the newly married pair. It was a surprise, but Odalie had been warned in advance and had produced from somewhere a jug of wine. Madame

Aubert Rocque and her nieces came bearing cakes and bottles, and many of the young girls brought trinkets to the bride: handkerchiefs, bundles of dried *vertivert* for perfuming the clothes and linens in *armoires*, a gay patchwork quilt, jars of preserved fruits, a box of candied orange peel. And with them, the young people brought the fiddlers, two old men who had played at countless wedding celebrations.

It was gay in the Vidal house that evening as the boys and girls danced, and as they sat about in couples later with cake and wine. Yellow lamplight shone on the light-colored dresses of the girls and upon their black hair and flashing dark eyes. Many of the boys wore flowers, to show that they were courting, or romantically inclined. It was an old custom on Isle Brevelle to wear a flower thrust behind the ear. Numa had worn cape jasmine when he was courting Famie at Easter a year ago. Lately he had not thought of flowers, but tonight one of the girls put a white rose behind his left ear and Numa let it remain there, smiling across her shoulder at Famie, who sat admiring the small stitches and intricate quilting upon the patchwork coverlet. She returned his smile and put a sprig of honeysuckle into her hair.

At midnight the guests left, going in groups down the lane or through the fields, singing as they went. In the doorway Famie and Numa stood looking after them as they went through the moonlight on their way.

Odalie and Bizette went quietly into the other room where the child lay sleeping, and quietly they closed the door behind them.

The old men had instructed Numa as to his behavior on his wedding night, so he left Famie and went outside into the moonlight while she undressed and made ready for bed. The night was still and the moon was white in the dark sky; the river was so tranquil that stars reflected themselves in it. The boy sat on the bench under the China tree and looked at the familiar things around him, moon, river, sky, and sheltering tree. This was his home now and Famie was his wife. These acres would be added to his and they would one day belong to his children. He was a man now and must assume a man's responsibility ... That was what the priest had said.

And Famie would love him; she had promised today that she would do so in sickness and in health and forever. And now, tonight, she would be completely his own, dark hair, eyes, lips, heart, and body. He had waited so long and time had been cruel, but now she belonged to him as completely as he belonged to her.

He turned and looked at the house, and saw that she had put out the light.

From the pillow Famie saw his form darken the moonlit door. He came quietly into the room and passed into the shadow. A chair creaked as he sat upon it, and she heard him put down one shoe after another. Why was she afraid? Why did she dread this moment? A year ago she had lain in this very bed, counting the minutes until she could rise and cross the river to lie in the arms of her lover. Blind passion had urged her on. She would have tried to kill anyone who barred her way. And now, in the dark near-by, there was Numa — a friend but yet a stranger — and in a moment he would be beside her. No, it was too soon, the misery of her loss was too great. She could not . . .

She saw the body of the man black against the moon-lit door, and then she felt his body against hers, his hands on her breast, she felt his lips hot against hers. Why couldn't she move? Why did she lie there like a dead woman?

'Famie . . . Oh God, how Ah've waited . . . Famie . . . Ah love yo' . . . Love me, please . . . Oh God, Famie . . . please . . . please . . .'

His arms were around her, he was pressing quick, hot kisses on her lips, her breast. She shuddered.

' . . . please . . . please . . .'

And then, as his fingers caressed her cheek, he paused, feeling the tears upon her face. A pause as he lay quiet beside her, then his voice changed as he said in a tired whisper, 'It's . . . It's all right.'

She could not answer for the sob which choked her, but he felt her body tremble. He drew away from her and sat on the edge of the bed, his face buried in his arms. He felt as though an iron band was pressing on his forehead, and suddenly he was weak and tired. Nothing mattered any more.

After a long time he felt her hand on his shoulder and heard her husky whisper: 'I ... I'm sorry, Numa.'

He took her hand and laid it against his forehead: 'It's ... it's all right.'

The room was very still; they could hear the crickets in the grass on the river bank, and somewhere far away a dog bayed at the moon.

When Numa spoke again his voice was hoarse. 'It ... it don' make no difference ...'

## PART THREE

*THE BIG–HOUSE AND THE CABIN*

# CHAPTER XV

'FAMIE, I declare I don't believe that even the fine laundresses in New Orleans can do this delicate work as well as you do,' said Miss Adelaide. 'I'm glad you've decided to do my work again. I was afraid that you'd stop when you married, and I knew that Odalie couldn't do it without you.'

'No'm, I'm glad to have it to do,' said the girl, speaking carefully, as she always did when she talked to white people.

The two women stood beside the large four-post bed in the white-and-yellow bedroom at Yucca; on the counterpane the fine linen baby clothes were spread out for inspection.

Miss Adelaide was going to have another baby, and she wore a long white wrapper with ruffles and a short train. As she put down the last garment she said: 'I'll give you an order so you can get your money at the store. I haven't a cent in the house.'

She went to the table and took up pencil and paper, scribbled Famie's name and the amount, and handed the folded slip to the girl.

'Could I see little Guy?' the girl asked. 'He's the pretties' baby I ever did see.'

'Of course,' said Miss Adelaide, and without moving her head she shouted: 'Aunt Dicey! Oh, Aunt Dicey!' and as a reply came from a distant room, she shouted again: 'Bring the baby to me... Come a-jumpin'!'

Her voice was kind and gay. 'You know, I think he's pretty myself.' She laughed.

The old woman came into the room, nodded grudgingly to Famie, handed the baby to his mother, and went out without speaking a word.

'Don't pay any attention to that old crosspatch,' said Miss Adelaide, knowing Famie's embarrassment before this slight. 'She thinks she owns me and the baby too. Well, she'll have her hands full soon enough.'

She put the child down upon a chair and they stepped back to admire him.

'Now, Famie, you know that *is* a pretty child, even if I do say so myself!'

'Yes, ma'am, he sho' is.'

'Oh, he's a beautiful object!'

'Yes, ma'am.'

'Aren't you the prettiest child on Cane River?'

'Yes, ma'am, he sho' is.'

'Look at him. He's smiling; he knows all about it.'

'Yes, ma'am, he sho' does.'

As they spoke they continued to step backward, talking as much to the child as to each other.

'Prettiest baby in the . . .'

But at that moment, as they retreated together, they stumbled over a chair and both fell sprawling upon the floor.

Terrified that the white woman had hurt herself, Famie scrambled to her feet, but Miss Adelaide lay flat on the floor shrieking with laughter.

'Oh, I'm a plum fool!' she said as soon as she could speak. 'We're both fools, Famie. Oh, but my husband would laugh if he could see us.'

And she sat up, still laughing. The baby, pleased with the excitement, crowed and patted his hands.

Aunt Dicey heard the crash and came running into the room; she helped Miss Adelaide to her feet, quarreling all the while: 'Ah declare, Miss Adelaide, yo've got little to do, fallin' down *now*. S'pose yo' hu't yo'seff, an' s'pose yo' hu't . . .'

'Oh, hush up, old fussy-cat,' said Miss Adelaide, wiping her eyes, 'I didn't hurt myself nor the baby either. Go along and tell Mug to bring me some coffee. And tell her to fix an extra cup for Famie — she'll stop and get it on her way home.'

But Aunt Dicey, instead of answering, stood transfixed looking out of the window toward the front gate: 'Lawd Gawd, what's dat?' she cried.

Miss Adelaide looked and her voice was excited as she replied: 'Land sakes, Dicey, it's an automobile!'

'A what?' Aunt Dicey was so excited that she forgot to say 'ma'am.'

'An automobile, a horseless carriage,' said Miss Adelaide, 'and it's the very first one I've ever seen on Cane River. How in the world did they ever get all this way from town over those old broken bridges and narrow roads? It's hard enough to get to town in the surrey . . .' She broke off and said: 'Come along, let's all go and see who it is. Here! Take the baby, Aunt Dicey. Come along, Famie. Hurry!' And she was off downstairs, her train rustling behind her on the steps.

A strange-looking machine stood panting and smoking before the door; its wheels had torn up great patches of grass from the drive. It was rather like a surrey, except that it had no top. On the high front seat sat a man, and a woman covered completely in a brown linen duster; the woman's hat was swathed in a long floating veil. The man sat beside her with his hands on the steering wheel, and he appeared tired.

The woman jumped down from the high seat and embraced Miss Adelaide. 'Darling!' she cried. 'I haven't seen you in *ages!*'

'Why, Flossie Whitney, it's been six years . . . Lord, but I'm glad to see you. And you've got an automobile.'

'Darling, *darling* Adelaide. Oh, I want you to meet my husband. My *dear*, didn't you know? I'm married — yes, married. And his name's Smith. Isn't that *terrible?*'

'I thought you were going to say his name was Andrew Carnegie,' said Mr. Guy, who had come up the drive, a crowd of curious negroes and mulattoes at his heels.

'Why, Guy Randolph! Mr. Randolph, this is my husband, Harold Smith. Isn't it a *common* name? And he won't even let me call him *that*. Everybody calls him Harry. You might as well call him that too. Adelaide, darling... You've got one baby and you're going to have *another* one. Isn't that *grand?* I've only got an automobile and two dogs. Fortunately, I didn't bring the dogs today. We broke down three times on the way, and we went through a bridge too. My dear, I was scared to *death*. Harry, I didn't introduce you to Adelaide. You know all about her. We were at school together. You remember, don't you, all the things I told you about her? Of *course* you do. Adelaide, darling, may I come inside and wash? I expect to stay days and *days* with you... I'll probably spend the summer.'

The group moved toward the door of the sitting-room, and as Mrs. Smith caught sight of herself in the mirror just inside the door she screamed afresh: 'My dear! Why didn't you *tell* me? My hair! It looks like a *rat's* nest.' She was still talking as the door closed.

Mug the cook, Henry-Jack the yard man, and Famie stood with a group of negroes at one side of the car, looking, admiring. 'Ah swear, Ah can't see what make it go,' said Henry-Jack, and his wife replied: 'Nigger, it ain't none o' yo' business what make it go. Dat's white folks' worriment. An' anyhow I got to go an' see after my dinner.' She shuffled off toward the kitchen.

'You ought to buy one of these Autocars,' said Mr. Smith to Mr. Randolph. 'Out here in the country it would be a big help to you. Why, you can go to town in just a couple of hours — or you could, rather, if the roads were better and the bridges were fixed up.'

Mr. Randolph said: 'Don't say that to my wife, or she'll be wanting one. As far as I'm concerned, I'd rather have a good horse than the best automobile made.'

'That's what I said at first,' said the other. 'But you'd be surprised at the number of automobiles that you see on the streets in New Orleans these days. There must be seventy-five or a hundred in the city.'

'Well, that's all right for you city people,' said Mr. Guy, 'but I'd like to see you try to navigate these river roads after a rain. I'll tell you this: if it rains today, you and your wife will spend a long time with us. We'd be glad to have you, too. It's pretty lonesome out here for Adelaide. I'm so busy and there's so much to do running the plantation that I don't have time to get bored, but Adelaide hasn't a woman friend within ten miles.'

'Ten miles! Good lord, Randolph, there must be some people closer than that. It looks like a well-populated rural community.'

'They're all colored people,' said Mr. Guy. 'We're just a white island in the Black Sea.'

'But I saw lots of people who looked . . .'

'Yes, I know,' said Mr. Guy. 'But those are the mulattoes. This is the center of their settlement. There must be two thousand of them living in the vicinity. And there are a lot of negroes too; about three hundred or more negroes live right here on Yucca.'

'That's interesting. I didn't know that there was such a community here,' said Mr. Smith. 'You must tell me about it; I'm curious.'

'Later on,' said Mr. Guy. 'I expect it must be nearly dinner time. Let's go in and join the womenfolks.'

But at that moment the ladies joined them.

'We'll just have to wait awhile for dinner. The automobile has demoralized the servants. I went in the kitchen, and there was the gumbo boiling over, all over the stove.'

Miss Adelaide didn't seem to mind at all. 'Lord, I'm glad to see you again, Flossie, and to meet your husband. And now you must explain the automobile to me. I've never ridden in one.'

'My dear, we shall take you for a ride right after dinner. We'll take you *miles* in just no time at *all*. It's perfectly grand. Mr. Randolph, you ought to buy

Adelaide an automobile. I haven't learned to drive one yet, but I'm going to. Harry doesn't *trust* me. Isn't that terrible? He says that I'd run the machine up a tree. But he doesn't mean it; and besides that, who is *he* to talk? Didn't I sit there like a regular *Spartan* when he ran right into the *ditch?* But I declare, Adelaide, it just breaks my heart when we run over chickens. They just *won't* get out of the way. They just *stand* there. We killed *dozens* on the way out here. Really, I lost count. I just sat there and *yelled* at them: Skiddoo! Skiddoo! That's the latest slang expression, darling — everybody says it all the time. But the chickens wouldn't skiddoo, so we ran over them, hundreds!'

'We ran over one, to be exact,' said Mr. Smith, laughing.

'Well, perhaps it *was* only one, but we *nearly* killed hundreds more. And Mr. Randolph, I think it's a shame for you to keep Adelaide just *buried* out here on the plantation. I want to have her come and visit me in town. Everybody is playing a new game called Flinch now. Addie, you'd love it. Who's that girl over there?'

Famie had been standing listening to the conversation. She had never heard so much white folks' talk in all her life. She didn't understand half of it, but it was fascinating. She started guiltily as Mrs. Smith pounced upon her.

'That's Famie Vidal, who washes the baby's clothes,'

said Mr. Guy. 'She is one of the mulattoes that I've been telling Smith about.'

'Oh . . . a mulatto? I can hardly believe it. Do come here and let me look at you. Why, you could pass for white anywhere . . . nearly anywhere. Adelaide, she's far too pretty. If I were you I wouldn't have her on the place. No, now don't go away just because I said that. I didn't intend to hurt your feelings. I was giving you a compliment. Well, I suppose I shouldn't have said it — she's probably shy. I didn't intend to drive her off . . . My dear, what was I saying? Oh yes, I know. Adelaide, you must, you really must get your husband to buy you one of these new piano-players. They're wonderful. They play better and faster and louder than *anybody* can play by hand. Yes, Adelaide, you really must get your husband to buy you a pianola.

'Heavens above, what am I talking about? Guy, I've got the most *wonderful* news for you. You don't mind my calling you Guy, do you? Call me Flossie, of course. I can't stand formality when I'm in the country, and besides, I've known Adelaide all my life. What was I saying? Oh, yes, who *do* you think I saw in New Orleans? Your brother Paul. He had just come home from *France* or somewhere. Yes, of course, Paul. Didn't you know he was *back?* He's taking some sort of treatment. He's sick. Oh, not very sick, I think, but there's something wrong. And he's back in the United States to *stay*. He told me so himself. He's coming *here*. We tried to get him to come with us, but he wouldn't. You know how Paul is; he hasn't changed a bit. Hasn't he written to you? How ridiculous! You'd think you were strangers instead of being brothers. Adelaide, my dear, he's famous. His pictures are hanging in the Metropolitan Museum and goodness knows where else. He sent you all sorts of messages, only I've forgotten them. But I do remember this: he's coming *here*. He said he'd be here one day next week. There's the dinner bell. Good. I'm simply *starving*. Darling, it's wonderful for you to let us come bouncing in on you like this. You haven't the least idea what a terrible time we had getting here.'

# CHAPTER XVI

HENRY TYLER was a field-hand who lived on Yucca plantation. He was a big black man, strong as an ox, humble as a mule. His eyes asked questions. He was born on the place and had never been more than twenty miles away from it in his life. His wife was a fat, loud-mouthed woman with gold hoops glittering in her ears; she shouted at his four black sons, sang louder than any one else in the African Baptist church, and 'meddled' Henry when he was studying things in his mind.

When there's fighting in the big-road you can run home, the old folks say, but what are you going to do when the fighting is in your own cabin?

Henry plowed the east field day after day, year after year. Up and down, slowly, behind his mule and plow. It was known as Henry's field, although of course it belonged to Mr. Guy, the white owner of the two thousand acres that made up the plantation. Henry, in a sense, belonged to Mr. Guy just as the land did.

Along the edge of the field the river drowsed in the sun, choked with purple water-lilies, its bank covered with a thicket of trees and vines. Birds made their nests there undisturbed and green lizards and black turtles sunned themselves on half-submerged logs. From the trees long streamers of gray moss hung down, like old men dipping their beards into the water.

Sometimes Henry would stop at the end of a furrow, his head thrown back, his eyes staring into the distance. He wanted something. He couldn't say what it was exactly, but the ache was there. Standing behind his plow he would try to pray:

'Please, Jesus . . .'

Then he would stop. How can Jesus give a man something when the man doesn't know what he is asking for? Henry would flick the reins against the flanks of his mule as it waited in the simmering sun. 'Git up, mule!' he would say.

Up and down the field, slowly, day after day.

The negroes all said that Mr. Guy's brother had come home to die. This was the principal topic on the store gallery at night when the black men loafed, watching the round red moon untangle itself from the trees and rise above its reflection in Cane River.

His name was Mr. Paul. When he was young he had

lived on the plantation too, but that was all of fifteen years go. He had been different from Mr. Guy, the older son of the old planter, even then — sickly-like and puny from the time he was a baby. Why, Uncle Chawlie could remember him well — a spindling little boy, lying on the floor of the gallery of the big-house painting with water-colors, or leaning back against one of the tall white columns reading a book.

Guy, his brother, had been the very spit of his father — diving from high trees into the river, or riding wild horses and rampaging over the country. Later on, when the older boy came home from the State University, he took hold of the place and ran things his own way. When the old planter died you hardly missed him. But Paul had gone away, up North, to lots of different places, and then had gone to live over with foreign people somewhere. The negroes had almost forgotten about Mr. Paul until his return. There had been excitement then, for Mr. Paul was mighty sick — coughing all the time and having fever. Tuberculosis it was. Lots of niggers die of it too. It's bad.

But Mr. Paul seemed to make a joke of it. For instance, he was contrary-minded, and insisted that he would not live in the big-house with Mr. Guy's wife and child — said the disease was catching. Instead he had taken an empty nigger cabin nearly half a mile away from the dwelling of the white people, had gone there directly after his arrival, and had stayed there ever

since, all by himself. Sometimes he painted at a big
easel outdoors, under the blossoming Chinaball tree. He
had been home a month now, and folks had got used to
meeting a negro house-man riding on horseback from
the big-house, balancing a tray of smoking dishes, or
carrying a coffee-pot in one hand — galloping his horse
so the food would still be hot when he got there.

That was about all Uncle Chawlie knew, but he asked
the others. Aunt Dicey, who worked for the white folks
at Yucca, went over sometimes and cleaned the cabin,
scrubbed the floors, and waited on Mr. Paul. She told
stories about solid gold hairbrushes, and lots of things
she didn't even know the names of — but who could
believe that old woman? A natural-born liar, that's
what she was, and always trying to be important in
what she knew about white folks' doings. Nevertheless,
it was true about the silk clothes; Uncle Chawlie had
seen them himself, flopping in the breeze on the clothesline: 'Hones' to Gawd, yo' wouldn' believe!'

Henry, lolling on his elbow in the dark near-by, puffed
deep on his pipe and said: 'I sometimes sees him when
I'm plowin' de eas' fiel' . . . Looks powerful sick tuh me
. . . but 'e always say, "Howdy," friendly-like an' nice.'

Uncle Chawlie 'lowed Henry could tell a lot more,
but he was one of those shut-mouth niggers, no good at
talking — just studying to himself all the time. The
matter dropped. The black men yawned, whistled to
their cur dogs, and disappeared one after the other in

the shadows, riding their sleepy horses toward cabins dotted along the river bank. But Henry sat on, alone in the moonlight, scratching his yellow dog between its ears and thinking about Mr. Paul. Funny thing about your thoughts — you don't know why they keep on running on things that way. Why, once Henry had got a tune in his head — a baptizing tune — and it stayed there for four days and four nights until he almost lost his mind. Now Mr. Paul was on his mind, just like that tune.

The cotton rows were very long, running all the way across a wide point that jutted out into the river. At the lower end of the field was Henry's house, and at the upper end of the furrow, the cabin where Mr. Paul lived nowadays. From far off, as he walked behind his plow, Henry could see the turkey-red curtains blowing out in the breeze, and the white man lying back in a big chair in the doorway, reading a book, or just sitting there looking out. His figure danced up and down in the heat waves which swam over the furrows. Mr. Paul wore a purple silk dressing-gown nearly all the time, bright and gay. He liked the same colors that Henry did.

Sometimes Mr. Paul painted at a big picture out under the Chinaball tree before the cabin. Henry couldn't see what he was painting, couldn't guess. He wondered, though. Mr. Paul was thin and small, not big like his brother. He had quick hands and red lips and a lot of black hair. From a little way off he looked a boy and moved about like one, delicate-like and soft.

His hand trembled the day he gave Henry a glass of lemonade through the high wire fence which divided the cabin yard from the cotton field. Henry had been surprised. Mr. Guy would never have done that — or at least not in that way. Mr. Paul had a big glass pitcher of lemonade on a table just inside the door, and when he saw Henry and his mule approaching down the long furrow he poured out a glassful and walked into the sunlight, bareheaded, handing it to him through the meshes of the fence. Henry stood on the other side and drank. Lord, but it was good! Nice and cool and satisfying. It didn't seem to satisfy Mr. Paul, though, for he had hardly tasted it.

When Henry was through drinking, Mr. Paul gave him a cigarette as long as a cigar and lighted a match for him. Their hands touched and Mr. Paul's hand was cold... That's what sickness does to you. You can feel Old Death coming.

Henry was mighty sorry for Mr. Paul. Wished he could do something. 'Is yo' feelin' betta today, suh?' he said, and the white man answered: 'Yes, I'll be well soon. I like the heat. I had forgotten how good it feels to be warm.'

He said other things too, harder to understand. About the plowed land he talked, and about the mules and niggers and growing cotton: 'A man forgets these things in cities ... This is what I need. Simple things, like you, Henry — your plow and your mule and this good black earth with green things growing in it.'

Yes, sir, that's what sickness does to you. Sickness comes on horseback but it goes away on foot. Mr. Paul had fever right that minute, and when white folks are sick they always seem sicker than niggers ... they look sicker.

Henry began feeling sorrier and sorrier for Mr. Paul. Every time he came down the long furrows he looked and looked. The eyes of the two men met, held, until Henry turned his mule and plow around, and went back again.

When he came down the third row, Mr. Paul said: 'Come and sit under the tree, Henry, and talk to me for a few minutes. Guy won't mind — I'll tell him.'

Henry looked up and down the wire fence. It was very high, two full widths of woven hog-wire. There was not a hole in it anywhere. It stretched out nearly half a mile, past the orchard, past the vegetable patch, clear to the edge of the flower-garden of the big-house. Two years ago old Uncle Isaac, who lived in the cabin then, had been given the care of Mr. Guy's fine game chickens. Game chickens can fly high and are much too valuable to be stolen by niggers. The fence was to protect them. The chickens were gone now, gone like poor old Uncle Isaac, but the barrier remained.

Back of the cabin the long, empty chicken-runs

stretched out almost to the river bank; at the end of these, the fence turned at a right angle and continued away from the cotton field a quarter of a mile or more until it joined the picket fence around the stables and mule lot. To get to the cabin from the field you had to walk clear up to the big-house, where Mr. Guy sat in his 'office.' An explanation would be due for leaving your mule and plow. Mr. Paul couldn't get out into the field or to the river bank, and Henry couldn't get into the cabin yard. Henry had to explain all this to Mr. Paul, because he didn't want the white man to think him unthankful for his offer. He went off behind his mule again, trying to make up his mind to ask the white man to let him come over some evening instead. Mr. Paul could tell him things he wanted to know, about men in faraway places, and cities.

But there was that fence. It was so high, and you couldn't cross it without breaking it down. And you couldn't do that, of course. Henry found it hard to talk through the wire. It got into the way of what you were trying to say. Besides, it is mighty hard to say things to white folks so they can understand you.

There were two questions Henry wanted to ask. If anybody in this world could answer them, it was Mr. Paul. Why was it that Henry couldn't get on, couldn't better himself? Why was it that he had to work, just like this old mule, day after day until he died? Stuck, like a fly in molasses. Henry wanted to learn *too* bad.

But everything hindered him. His wife laughed and shouted, or got mad and burned up his books. She taught her four black sons to laugh too. 'Nigger is nigger,' she said, mocking him, shaming him before people. But that wasn't true, and Henry knew it.

He sighed and bent his head over the plow. 'Git up, mule,' he said. The beast strained forward under the weight of the heavy soil.

Up and down the field, slowly. Furrow after furrow.

It took him three days to get up enough courage to talk again to Mr. Paul, and maybe he wouldn't have talked even then, but the white man came out to the fence to give him another of those long, good-smoking cigarettes. This time they talked of the picture Mr. Paul was painting. Henry wanted to see what it was, so Mr. Paul turned it around. Henry could see it was a stretch of cotton field, with a plow and a nigger coming along — Mr. Paul had put him in a picture without Henry's knowing a thing about it. That was a strange thing, too. Henry couldn't see the picture very well because it was some distance from him, but he could see what it was. He was pleased and proud. This was something to tell the black men on the store gallery tonight. But some way, when the time came, he couldn't do it, even when the conversation turned to the sick man again.

People had come all the way from town to see Mr. Paul, but he had refused to see them, according to kitchen gossip — just wouldn't be bothered. 'An' he's sure one sp'iled white man,' Uncle Chawlie concluded.

'Huh! It wuz swellin' up whut bust de poutin' pigeon!' came the comment from a shapeless black shadow at his elbow.

''E ain't sp'iled! 'E ain't proud!' Henry startled them all with the passion of his reply. ''E's a sick man, dat's whut 'e is!'

But Uncle Chawlie said only 'Aie-yie!' a comment which can mean anything or nothing. There was a long silence broken by the whining of mosquitoes and the stamping of the sleepy horses tied to the railing. Henry rose, whistled to his cur dog, and started home.

Across the narrow river the lights in the cabins were winking out, one after another.

The next night Henry didn't go to the store to loaf and visit with the other men. Instead he sat by the smoky oil lamp in his cabin and tried to read from a book he had. His wife and children, already in bed, called out impatiently for him to put out the lamp, but Henry paid no heed. He wanted to learn to read better. Things came so hard. It was harder to read than plow, and he was tired already from the day's plowing. But it was nice to look out along the furrows and see the light in Mr. Paul's cabin. Mr. Paul was reading too.

It was the next night that Henry went out alone for the first time. His wife's nagging voice worried him more than usual:

'Fo' Gawd's sake put out dat lamp, Henry! De room is full o' mosquitoes dis minute. T'row dat ole fool book away an' lemme git some res'!'

Henry rose, blew out the lamp, and went outdoors. The yellow dog, lying in the dark by the side of the house, beat his tail on the hard-baked ground. For a while Henry sat on the steps watching the light that glimmered in the cabin across the field. There was a light in the parlor of the big-house too, tonight. Company there. He wondered if Mr. Paul had walked over to spend the evening, for once he had seen him walking through the orchard late at night after leaving the big-house. But that was a month ago. Mr. Paul seldom walked nowadays.

Finally Henry began to walk down the rows that he had plowed that day. The light in Mr. Paul's house urged him on. Maybe the white man was sick and needed something.

When he came to the high fence he stopped and peered. Mr. Paul was nowhere in sight. Henry walked along the fence a little way and tried to look in at the open windows. From where he stood now he could see nearly all of the lighted room, but Mr. Paul was nowhere in sight. Maybe he had fallen to the floor and was lying there, too weak to get up.

And then out of the darkness came a quiet voice: 'Is it you, Henry?'

'Yassuh!... I jus'...'

But there were no questions. Mr. Paul seemed to think it was the most natural thing in the world for Henry to be there at this time of night. He said: 'If you'll go along the fence to the big-house, you'll find the gate unlocked, I expect. Come on in.'

'No suh, not tonight... I jus' come...' Henry paused. He couldn't say why he had come.

Mr. Paul got out of the hammock under the China-ball tree and came close. 'I'm going to get a pair of pliers from the store tomorrow,' he said, 'and make a hole in that fence.'

But the next day Mr. Paul was in bed. The doctor came all the way out from town to see him and he stayed a long time. Mr. Guy and his wife, looking worried, were at the cabin too. When Henry came close to the fence with his mule and plow at midday, Mr. Guy came out and called him, telling him to run quick to the store and bring something. Henry didn't know what he went for, as Mr. Guy had written it on a piece of paper, but the clerk in the store whistled when he read it and gave Henry a small package. 'Looks bad,' the clerk said.

That night Mr. Guy sat up in the cabin until after midnight, and when he went, Aunt Dicey was left to watch. It was nearly daylight before Henry slipped into bed beside his wife, his overalls covered with dirt from the furrows in which he had lain for hours, on guard.

But it was not so serious after all, for in a few days Mr. Paul was out in the hammock again. He hadn't forgotten either.

'I've ordered those pliers,' he said. 'I'm going to cut a hole in that fence.'

Henry went back to the store gallery that night to loaf and visit with the men again. He was more silent than usual. He lay back against one of the posts, scratching the dog between the ears and puffing on his pipe. It was cooler here than in his cabin. And the river smelled so nice.

When he left, he rode home in a roundabout way through the field in order to pass Mr. Paul's cabin and see in at the windows from his position on horseback. There was a light burning, but the white man was nowhere in sight. The hammock flopped empty in the breeze and the moonlight made all the cabin yard visible. Henry ventured to call out softly: 'Oh, Mister Paul!' but there was no reply.

He rode along a little way. His beast shied suddenly and stumbled. A piece of wire had tripped his old white horse. A hole had been cut in the fence and the wire bent outward, into the field.

Had Mr. Paul gone out, through the furrows, down to the bank of the river?

Henry rode out to see. The bank was full of cactus and flowering yucca. Young Chinaball trees grew on the incline which led down to the water in which the moon was mirrored. The air was heavy with the sweet breath of night-blooming jasmine.

Silhouetted against the sky, Henry sat on his horse and looked out over the rippling river. Opposite, dark cabins dotted the bank. Nothing moved. And then, quietly, came a voice: 'Henry . . . Is that you?'

'Yassuh!' Henry slipped down from the saddle and went quickly to the river's edge.

'You'll have to help me — I'm not strong enough to climb back into the boat.'

Of all things! Poor Mr. Paul had tried to swim. He was clinging now to a rowboat which swung clear of the bank just beyond the shadow of a clump of elderberry trees dripping with white flowers. Mr. Paul's head and one arm were visible, his arm clinging to the boat.

Henry tried first to reach the boat from the bank, but it was too far out. He slipped off his shirt and shoes and plunged in, sinking to his knees, at first, in the soft mud of the river's bottom. He reached the boat after a few rapid strokes, steadied it, and climbed in. The boat shipped water as he lifted the limp body of Mr. Paul from the river. Mr. Paul was breathing fast and his eyes were big and black. He lay naked in the moonlight, shivering, clutching Henry's arm with both hands. Finally he spoke.

'I couldn't have lasted ... five minutes ... longer, Henry. It's lucky for me ... you came. If you want to call it luck.'

'Oh, Mister Paul, yo' is too sick to try to swim. You might a-drowned yo'se'f ... Gawd! What ud Mister Guy say den?'

Moonlight turned the wet shoulders of the black man to bronze. He sat erect, one arm supporting the head of the other man.

Two men, one white, one black, in a boat on a still river. Nobody else, everybody asleep, and the world saturated with moonlight.

Henry felt as though he, too, were sleeping. 'Mister Paul ... yo' is goin' to catch col' lyin' heah ...'

'It doesn't matter ... Don't move. Stay here quietly and let me rest for a while ... Don't let me cough ...'

The boat drifted slowly, came closer to the bank, and rested finally in the deep shade of the trees. Beyond the shadow the moonlight turned the water into hundreds of shiny ripples. The scent of the jasmine hung in the air, sickeningly sweet. From fig trees across the river came the clear crowing of a cock, repeated a moment later by distant challenges. Again. Again. Then silence.

The white man spoke. 'Stars are pretty things, aren't they, Henry?'

Henry knew he must answer. It was bad for Mr. Paul to talk. He made a great effort.

'Yassuh. Sittin' in my do'way night-times I often

watches stars. De ole folks say dat when de Big Dipper tips 'way up, like it is tonight, dat rain is comin'. De crops need rain, Mister Paul.'

'Yes — rain.' He was making an effort to breathe quietly. 'What else do the stars tell you, Henry?'

'Well, suh, de ole folks say dat yo' can read yo' future in de stars. But me, I don't know. Is dat true, or is it jus' a way a-sayin' things?'

The white man was coughing now. Not coughing hard, but somehow he didn't seem able to stop. Finally he made an effort to sit up, then fell limp against the black man's shoulder.

'Strange... The air is miles high, they say... It runs away up... and stretches all around us... but I don't seem able to get enough...'

'Lemme tek' yo' home, Mister Paul!'

'Not yet... Let me rest and ——'

'Please, suh...'

'It isn't often that two men are alone like this in a boat on a river at night... Here, in the dark, we are ourselves... like two shadows talking...'

'Please, suh... I can feel yo' heart beatin' and bangin'...'

' ... like two shadows talking... I can't feel my body any longer. I can only feel your strength holding me up ...' His voice became stronger. 'It has always been like this in the South... I mean, white men leaning on black men... from the beginning. We made slaves of

you; we made you work for us ... You made us rich ...
In rising, we pushed you further away from us ... And
yet, the system failed somehow ... Not only the war and
freeing the slaves ... Something else.'

'Yassuh ...?'

'Black men began to think, to move about, to go
away ... Why, you'll go away, Henry ... Or if not you,
your children. Do you want to go? To see things, to
learn things?'

'Oh, yassuh, I want to go *too* bad ...'

Now it was Henry who was breathless. He couldn't
talk. He was like an animal trying to tell a man it is
thirsty.

'It's come to me tonight. You and I stand for something that no longer exists — I mean that you came
when I needed you. Your strength supports me. I can
feel your strength. Do you see? You have everything
that I want in life — simplicity, health, and — interest
in living. I no longer want anything.

'But it was something else that I wanted to say. I
— I am like this land. When your strength is taken
away, I shall live no longer. Weeds will grow in the
furrows, the fields will go back to the brush. Henry!
This is why I couldn't get you out of my mind as I
watched you sweating in the field — working for something that can never be yours because I have taken it
from you.'

The negro tried to speak, but Mr. Paul went on talk-

ing. 'I can see now that I must help you. I can help
you if you will let me. Tomorrow I will take you from
the field, take you to work for me. Your wages will go
on, but I will teach you ... I can give you your chance.
Will you come?'

'I — I'd be *too* glad. Yo' cain't mean it, suh ...?'

'Yes, I can give you something to go forward on. But
I can't give you happiness, because I don't know what
happiness is. It may be that when you sit in your doorway looking at the stars you are as happy as man was
meant to be ... I am happier now, this moment, than
when I first knew success. But no! I must not tell you
that. What I mean is this: I am happy now. Do you
see? One friend came when I needed him most.'

'You don't mean me, Mister Paul?'

'Yes, you, Henry — like brothers, maybe ——'

'Please suh, yo' is cold. Lemme tek' yo' in.'

'Not yet. How sweet the jasmine smells — everything is rustling and moving about — the moon is ...'

'Oh, Mister Paul, lemme carry yo' home. I'm
afraid.'

'Soon, Henry, soon. I'll be better in a little while.'

'I can carry yo' easy, suh!'

'I'm heavy, Henry.'

'No, suh, yo' don' weigh nuthin'.'

Catching at the overhanging boughs of the trees,
Henry pulled the boat to shore and carried Mr. Paul up
the bank, along the cotton rows, and to the wire fence.

The yellow dog followed close at Henry's heels and the white horse raised his head.

Stooping, he put Mr. Paul through the opening in the fence, then crawled in afterward. The light was still burning in the cabin. The negro put the white man on the bed gently, wiping dry his feet, and covering him with a quilt. Mr. Paul lay with closed eyes. He was breathing easier now.

The black man stood looking about the cabin, looking at Mr. Paul's silver-backed hairbrushes, at the pictures turned with their faces to the wall. One of those canvases was the picture of Henry and his mule. Tomorrow morning, like the picture, Henry would belong in this cabin with Mr. Paul. He felt very thankful. Now he knew what he wanted to pray for: 'Please, Jesus . . .'

But what was he thinking of, standing there like that? He must go and get Mr. Paul's clothes and his own. This was his job now, waiting on the white man, learning things from him. Ahead of him he saw happy years. Learning things. Going North. Seeing cities.

He went back to the river bank and picked up Mr. Paul's robe and slippers from the grass. The yellow cur had followed him and was running about, snapping at fireflies on the slope. Henry spoke to the cur happily: 'We got us a new boss now, dawg!'

The dog darted on ahead, his tail erect, and ducked through the hole in the fence just as though he knew he were welcome at white folks' houses. Henry followed, holding the robe carefully away from the sharp ends of the broken wire. The dog was at the cabin door, standing in the lamplight, looking in. One forepaw was raised. He sniffed the air.

Then he raised his head and whined, retreated into the shadow and bayed — a long, mournful howl.

Henry stopped short, his eyes wide, his breath indrawn. Suddenly he shivered, for, from far off, another dog had answered.

And then, from distant cabins, from beyond the river, and from down the lane came the howling of other dogs — as faint and as final as death cries heard in a dream.

# CHAPTER XVII

IT WAS eleven o'clock at night when Mr. Guy, returning from a meeting of neighboring planters in Cloutierville, rode up to the commissary at Yucca. The negroes
had all gone home and no one was waiting to take his
horse, so he dismounted at the store gallery, took off the
saddle and bridle, and opened the gate to the mule lot.
The sweating horse brushed by him as it went to the
water trough beyond the hayracks. Mr. Guy sighed; he
was tired and discouraged, and the meeting had worn
him out. Sometimes, he thought, the best of us do the
stupidest things; for hours the group had talked, yet
nothing constructive had come into the discussion of a
better way to handle share-croppers, and sooner or later
something had to be done.

His irritation was aggravated when he discovered
that he had forgotten his keys. The saddle must be put

into the commissary; he couldn't leave it lying on the gallery. Perhaps, he thought, the clerk was still awake, and could take the saddle into his room overnight. The planter walked around the corner of the building and went to the back of the commissary to the room where the clerk slept. Despite the warm night, the door and window were closed tight. His hand was raised to knock when he heard a woman's voice in the dark room. So that was it. He let his hand fall and stood staring at the closed door; then he rapped sharply and called: 'Come around to the front gallery. Hurry. And bring the keys with you.'

He felt the veins tighten in his neck as he strode away over the dewy grass. As he waited he walked up and down on the porch, his spurs jingling against the boards.

Presently the clerk appeared, wearing trousers and undershirt; he was barefoot and he carried the bunch of keys in his hand. He was hoping that Mr. Guy hadn't heard anything, and he was prepared to lie if necessary.

'You're late,' he commented, and he unfastened the padlock and let down the iron bar which fastened across the double doors.

'Put the saddle inside,' said Mr. Guy, 'and get a lantern.'

Now the clerk was sure that Mr. Randolph knew, but he did as he was told and locked the doors again.

'Can I do anything else for you?' he asked, his voice half brazen, half afraid.

'Yes — sit down!'

The clerk dropped down on the bench and Mr. Guy continued to walk to and fro.

'Thursday's the first of the month,' he said. 'I'll get someone to take your place by that time. I'll give you your wages tomorrow and I'll expect you to be gone from here by night. The overseer can take charge until I get another clerk.'

'Now, look here,' the clerk said, trying to overcome his fear. 'You ought not to fire me like that. I ain't done nothing. What grounds have you got for running me off like I was one of the niggers?'

Mr. Guy turned on him and the clerk fell back on the bench, afraid for a moment that the other would strike him.

'I told you when you came here that I wouldn't stand for your fooling with the negroes,' Mr. Guy said. 'Now don't lie to me or try to explain. I heard a woman's voice in your room just now when I went there to get the keys. No, I wasn't spying on you. But you understood when you came here that I felt that way ... Oh yes, I know that these things happen all the time, but I tell you I won't have it on Yucca. I'm like my father in that. And if a son of mine ever fooled with a colored woman I'd send him off, just as I'm sending you.'

'But ...' the clerk said.

'I'm not asking you to leave,' Mr Guy said. 'I'm telling you to go.'

Far off a dog howled.

Famie and Numa had remained late at his mother's house, and the stars told them that it was past eleven o'clock when they started home. The baby slept in Famie's arms. Because the road was lighter than the path through the field they came that way, and were nearly at the commissary when they heard Mr. Guy's voice raised in anger. They stopped in the deep shade of a tree and listened.

'Well, what did you expect me to do?' the clerk asked, gathering his courage. 'You don't know what it means lying up there in that hot little room night after night with nothing but mosquitoes to keep you company. I'm a man, Mr. Guy, and I've got a man's feelings. You ain't above drinking with the mulattoes yourself...'

'It's not quite the same thing,' Mr. Guy said. 'And you're not the first clerk that I've lost this way. I try to get married men, but it's not easy to do. The wives don't like it here; it's too lonesome for them, or else they get familiar with the niggers, and that won't do either.'

'It's all right to talk...' the clerk said, but Mr. Randolph interrupted him.

'Yes, I know it's lonesome here for you, but you took the job knowing that,' he said. 'But you could get married, or you could go to a white woman somewhere. I've got no patience with your kind. Now, I don't know who was in your room tonight, and I don't care, but I'll bet you one thing: that girl you had tonight was some decent little mulatto.  If you hadn't come along, she would have married one of her kind and everything would have been all right.  But she was poor and needed a dress or shoes or something you could give her, and so she came to you.  And now you've made a whore out of her . . . fourteen or fifteen years old probably.'

'Oh, I'm not the first man she's had . . .' the clerk said.

'Well, maybe not.  I don't know . . .' Mr. Guy's voice had gone flat, and he sat down heavily on the bench and began fumbling with the lantern.  'Listen to those damned dogs!'

'I never heard them howl like that before,' the clerk said.  'It gives me the creeps.  This whole damn country gives me the creeps.'

'About this girl,' Mr. Guy said.  'If you had let her alone, it's possible that she'd have married one of her own kind, and she would have been all right.  But you've fixed all that, probably.  A year from now I'll see a girl with a white baby, and one of the boys will whisper that it's yours . . . But you'll be gone from here . . .' His voice became ironic.  'They'll tell me that its father was just a white man passing through . . . a stranger.  Men like you take your pleasure but you won't take the responsibility.  As far as you're concerned, they're all children of strangers.'

In the shadow of the tree, Famie and Numa had heard every word.  He said in a whisper: 'Let me hold him,' as he took the sleeping child and put it against his shoulder and put his other arm around her. They walked forward together toward the commissary, both looking straight ahead. Perhaps they could pass without being seen.

'Those dogs are driving me crazy,' the clerk said.

Mr. Guy struck a match and lighted the lantern so that he could see his way to the big-house. Its light shone on the clerk's face; he looked frightened. The light fell, too, on Famie's white dress as she and Numa approached in the road.

'Who's that?' Mr. Guy called.

'It me . . . Numa Lacour.'

The moment of tension was broken; both white men were relieved.

'How are you, Numa?' asked the planter. 'Is that your wife with you?'

He walked toward them, holding his lantern high, but before Numa could answer a man's strangled shout was heard in the darkness: 'Mister Guy! Oh, Mister Guy . . .'

A second later a large negro stumbled into the circle of lantern light. His distorted face was ashen, he choked as he tried to speak. 'Oh, Mister Guy . . .'

'Who is it? I can't see. Is that you, Henry? What in God's name is the matter?'

The negro stumbled as though he were about to fall: 'Them dawgs . . .'

Famie stepped closer, intent on what the man was saying. Never had she seen a face so stricken, never had she seen a black man cry before.

The planter handed the lantern to the clerk and shook the negro by his shoulders. 'Talk! What is it? What's the matter with you, Henry? Answer me.'

The light flickered in the clerk's hand as Henry gasped: 'Quick! Come quick, Mister Guy ... It's yo' brother ... It's Mister Paul!'

# CHAPTER XVIII

'HE'S a fine chile,' said Madame Aubert Rocque, as she rocked back and forth by the open window, 'but he's too much pet.'

Famie bent over and touched a wet finger to the hot iron: psss . .t!

'Yo' dress him too good, yo' feed him too good, an' yo' spile him to death.'

Famie looked up and smiled at the old woman. 'Yo' spoil him yo'seff,' she said.

Although she was not more than twenty-three years old, she was beginning to stoop, and she was so thin that her dress hung in folds upon her. She stood now at the ironing-board, and in a basket beside her was a large pile of rough-dried children's clothes. She still washed for the children at Yucca, but there were four of them now; it took three full days to wash and iron all the things.

'How ole he is? I forgets.'

'Tell *Nainaine* how old yo' are, Joel,' she said.

The small boy in the doorway sat blowing bubbles with a small piece of bamboo cane. 'I'm six years ole,' he said, 'an' nex' yeah I'm goin' to school over yonder.' He pointed to the church and school beyond the river.

He was a handsome child, and there was nothing in his appearance to show that his mother was a mulatto woman; his eyes were clear and blue, and his red hair thick and straight. Famie loved him to the exclusion of everything else; he was hers and he was everything and nothing else mattered.

Madame Aubert started to speak, stopped, and asked another question. 'How come yo' name him Joel? Ah can' remember to save my life, an' yet I used to know.'

'He was a Christmas baby, don't you 'member?' Famie answered, as she continued to iron. 'Yo' was right here, yo' ought to know.'

'Yo' come near dyin' too,' said the old woman. 'An' yo' would have, ef it hadn' been fo' Numa...'

'Ah know,' said Famie. 'An' yo' an' Odalie wanted to name him Noel, and I wanted to name him Joe, fo' his papa. So we call him Joel, an' eve'ybody got satisfied.'

Madame Aubert put her handkerchief to her eyes. 'Po' sister,' she said. 'Po' Odalie. It make me plum sad jus' to come heah.'

Famie set her iron aside and went to put her arm

around the old woman's shoulder. 'Ah know. Seems to me eve'ything look diffe'nt since they ain't heah no mo'. Seems like Ah couldn't stan' it at first.'

Odalie and Bizette had died with pneumonia, one following the other within a week. It was three years ago now, but Famie felt the old, bitter sorrow. It had been so bad, and there was so little that she could do to help them. She thought of them now, lying side by side in the cemetery by the church, with their names black on the white wooden markers of their graves, and with the wreaths of immortelles already faded from rain and sun.

'Ah'll be goin' soon myself,' said the old woman.

'Ah, no, *Nainaine*, don't talk like that.'

'Ah'll be eighty years ole nex' August, Ah ain't got much time lef'.'

'Look, Mama!' cried Joel. A large bubble floated out into the sunlight, hung poised, disappeared.

'That's a fine one,' said the old woman, smiling as she wiped her eyes. 'Who taught yo' how to make them bubbles? Ah don' see no other little boys doin' that.'

'Mama, she showed me; she give me the cane, an' the soap, too. I got the cup an' water myself.'

Madame Aubert Rocque tied her black sunbonnet under her chin and went to the door. 'Ah got to be goin',' she said. 'Ah got to go an' help Numa's mama wid her quiltin'. Ah tole her Ah'd come befo' dinner, an' Ah got to go. That's a long piece fo' me to walk, an'

Ah didn' used to think it was but a step. Hey law! Lemme go.'

Numa's old clock struck eleven, and Famie started guiltily. 'Ah've got to start fixin' dinner myself,' she said. 'Numa goin' to be in from the fiel' befo' Ah know it.'

'How's he feelin'?' asked the old woman as she eased herself down from the porch to the ground.

'He's feelin' right good,' Famie answered, ''ceptin' he's so thin. He sweat at night, an' he cough a lot, but he say he feels good in de mawnin'.'

When the old woman had gone hobbling off down the road, Famie stirred up cornbread and set the molasses jug and the milk pitcher on the table. It was little enough, but it was all they had. She spoke to Joel, who had put aside his cane and was fishing with a straw down a hole in the ground. 'Seems to me Ah heard the hens cacklin', honey. Run out and see if yo' can't find some aigs fo' papa's dinner.'

'Aw, Mama, I don't want to. I'm fishin' fo' doodles.'

'Go on, Joel, and fin' me some aigs. Ah've got a su'prise fo' you after dinner.'

'What is it, Mama?'

'It's a new game that the little white boys plays at Yucca,' she said. 'Ah watched 'em, and Ah learned it good. After dinner, Ah'll show you. Yo' an' me, we're goin' to have fun. Hurry up now, and see if yo' can' fin' papa some aigs.'

In the field near the house Joel and some other mulatto children were playing a game. Numa and Famie, sitting relaxed yet weary on the moonlit porch, listened to the childish voices.

The little girls cried in chorus: '*What yo' make that fire for?*'

And the little boys, almost equally shrill: '*Kill me a chicken!*'

'*Whose henhouse yo' goin' get 'im out, mine or yo's?*'

'*Out o' yo's!*'

'*O-o-u!*' cried the little girls in fright, and then: '*Ah got the lock!*'

'*Ah got the key!*'

'*Yo' big-eyed witch, yo' ain't goin' to get my chickens!*'

'*Yo' little-eyed witch, Ah'm comin' to get yo' chickens!*'

Screams rang out as the game reached its climax, and the boys chased the girls through the field.


'We used to play that when we was child'en. 'Member, Famie?'

She nodded. 'Ah 'member good,' she said.

There was a pause, and then she said: 'Numa, the' ain't a piece o' firewood lef'. Ah split the las' pieces today. The res' is jus' chunks, an' Ah can' split 'em.'

He said: 'In the mawnin' Ah'll cut some.'

'It's too heavy fo' yo', Numa,' Famie said. 'Yo' lookin' so thin an' bad. Couldn' we get Henry Tyler to cut us some? He's big like a mule.'

'He's comin' here tonight,' Numa said. 'He wants to borrow ouh crosscut saw. Ah'll ask him. Maybe we can pay him somethin'... a chicken or a squab maybe...'

In the fields the children were chanting:

> Chick-a-ma, chick-a-ma cranie-crow,
> Went to the well to wash my toe.
> When Ah got back my chicken was gone.
> What time, ole witch?

Later Henry Tyler sat on the edge of the porch and talked with them. He would be glad to split all the wood that Miss Famie wanted, he said, he was that thankful for the loan of the saw. In the moonlight he seemed huge and black, and Numa seemed but a slim boy beside him.

Ever since the night when she and Numa met him crying in the road — that time when Mister Paul died and the dogs howled all night — Famie had watched him. From one of the windows she could see him as he plowed the east field at Yucca, just as she could see Numa plowing on their own land close by. She wondered what Henry thought about as he went up and down the long furrows, for on that night five years ago she had seen stark misery in his face, and, in that moment, she knew that his misery equaled her own. Not that she was unhappy any more; all of that was far behind her now, but she could not forget it.

Henry was talking about his life at Yucca; his voice was so low that it seemed that he talked to himself.

'It's been mo' than twenty yeahs since Ah been plowin' de eas' fiel' ... Ah work that place fo' Ah don' know how many days on one meal a day, and barefooted, in debt and my people all sick ... my chillen all small ... Ah use' to go sometimes an' sit an' talk wid ole Uncle Isaac who lived in that cabin where Mister Paul wuz ... Ah use' to sit an' talk wid Uncle Isaac an' Aunt Jane jus' fo' pastime ... an' tell 'em about my condition. Seems like it wuz so ha'd to 'cumulate a livin' fo' my fambly. Uncle Isaac use' to tell me 'bout how much betta he live in slavery time than he done since Surrender, since he wuz free. In them days, he say he had nothin' to worry him an' eve'thing wuz give to him. Ah still wonders about it.'

In the field the children were singing:

> Snakey bake a hoe-cake,
> Set a frog to mind it;
> Froggy got to noddin',
> Lizard come an' stole it.
> Bring back my hoe-cake, yo' long-tailed Nanny!

No matter how the games began, they always ended with screaming and running. Pretty soon, Famie said to herself, she must call the children in, send them home, and put Joel to bed. She looked at the stars: it was nearly eight o'clock.

Henry rose to go home. He put the crosscut saw

across his shoulder and the shiny blade glittered in the moonlight. 'Ah'll come soon in de mawnin' an' cut some wood fo' you, Miss Famie,' he said.

When he was gone, Famie said: 'Numa, please go see the doctor in town. Ah'm worried 'bout yo'. Ah heahs yo' coughin' in the night.'

'Ah'll go, fust chance Ah gets,' said Numa. 'But Ah'm all right, honey. Ah jus' ain't got no strength. Ah gets so ti'ed, so ti'ed.'

His voice was flat and hopeless. Famie knew what he was thinking about, although he had said nothing. He was thinking of Henry Tyler's four strong sons, boys who were all old enough to help pick cotton, and the oldest one could plow like a man. Numa wanted a son above everything else, and he knew now that he and Famie would never have one. Two years after their marriage Famie had given birth to a dead baby, and the doctor had said that she would never have another.

Numa blamed himself for this, for Joel was a fine, healthy child. But Joel was not his. Day by day Joel grew to look more and more like the red-haired man, the man Numa had helped to kill, and the blood money was still hidden in the clock-case on the mantel. How much did his mother know? Numa wondered. He thought of his marriage day, when his mother had come to Famie's house carrying the clock for a wedding gift; she had put it on the mantel and had set the pendulum swinging, just as it had swung at home. No, a man cannot get away from his sins, Numa thought; they follow him, like dogs.

But suddenly he remembered something, and said: 'Famie, Ah saw Nita today. She done come back.'

'No!' Famie cried.

'Ah saw her passin' in the road,' said Numa, 'lookin' jus' as young as the day she lef' heah five years ago. She didn' see me, or if she did, she didn' speak ... She jus' went ridin' by, on a spotted hoss.'

# CHAPTER XIX

EVERY negro for miles around Yucca plantation knew her, and when folks saw her striding along the road in her starched gray calico dress and black sunbonnet they would say: 'Yond' go Lizzie Balize.' But if she carried a basket covered with a white cloth, they would add: 'Aie-yie! Somebody sick 'roun' yeah.'

She nursed white and black alike; it was her business, and she could cure hysterical women just by a brew of herbs — her own concoction; but the women couldn't forgive her for curing them; it's awesome to be screaming and falling in fits — people coming from miles to see — but nobody pays attention if you are only vomiting, and that's what happened if Lizzie gave you her brew. Women didn't send for Lizzie Balize unless they were mighty sick.

She had little to do with the other negroes, and

hardly ever went to church. When she did go she sat up stiff and stern; she never shouted or clapped her hands or patted her feet like the others. She was too proud — though she was as black as anybody else, and ugly too. Her cheeks were spattered with white scars like rose petals, and she had a trick of passing her hand over her face as though she were trying to brush them away. Folks said they were the marks of smallpox.

She lived with her son on the bank of Cane River, about half a mile from the store. The cabin stood back from the road, and to get to it you had to walk a long way between the furrows. She had lived there twenty-five years, ever since she came first to the plantation, when Bull was nothing but a baby. Even old Aunt Dicey, washwoman for the white folks at the big-house, couldn't find out anything about her, and if Aunt Dicey couldn't there was no use asking about her. But she hadn't been at Cane River a year before folks got to know her as a sick-nurse and granny doctor. In spite of that she had few friends. She just didn't mix with folks; that was all there was to it.

Bull had grown to be a big lazy boy, as black as the back of the chimney, slow-moving and good-natured. It was his burly body that gave him the name, and he was proud of it. 'Dat ole boy is sho' built like a bull!' the other boys said when they went in swimming with him in the late afternoon.

But in spite of his fine body, Bull didn't care for

women.  True, he tripped up the girls in the furrows —
as the others did — and sometimes would go drinking
and sporting on Saturday night.  But usually you would
find him in the evening lying on the floor of Lizzie's
gallery in the shadow of the gourd vine — halfway
naked, halfway asleep, slapping at the mosquitoes that
whined over him.  And Lizzie just spoiled him to death,
folks said, waiting on him hand and foot, feeding him
like a fattenin' pig.  Just the same, even old Aunt Dicey
granted he was willing enough behind the plow, and the
little strip of land that Lizzie rented on shares from
Mr. Guy grew as much cotton as anybody's acres.

Sometimes Aunt Dicey would come over in the evenings and smoke her pipe in the moonlight on Lizzie
Balize's gallery, while Bull lolled on the floor humming
to himself.

'Funny 'e don' fool wid wimmin no',' Aunt Dicey
ventured.  As she rocked herself back and forth and
plied her black-bordered palmetto fan, Lizzie Balize
answered: 'Shucks, ole woman, Bull ain't got wimmin
on his mind.'

It was true enough.  Some of the nigger boys were
just like animals.  On Saturday nights you could hear
them howling and yelling in the fields, and you could
hear the girls squealing.  It was scandalous and a shame,
Aunt Dicey said, ignoring the fact that when she was
young she had screeched as loud as any of them.

Lizzie passed her black hand over the scars as though

to brush them away. 'It don't bother me none,' she said. She rocked back and forth and plied her fan against the mosquitoes. 'Yo' know, Dicey, the ole folks haz got a sayin' — Ah wonder ef yo' knows it. Dey say dat de 'ooman what looks for nassiness smells nasty. Better watch out!'

Dicey hoisted herself up from her chair and put her cold pipe into her apron pocket. 'How come yo' sass a 'ooman two times as ole as yo'?' she snorted. Then, when she had eased her heavy body down from step to step: 'It's dese heah shut-mouth, lazy, stay-at-home mens yo' got ter watch! Yo' jus' wait till de right gal come dis way and see how Bull goin' tuh behave! Ah've knowed sons smash down da' own mammies w'en dey got love-crazy.' And she walked to the gate grumbling to herself.

Lizzie sat rocking in the moonlight, moving her fan back and forth and looking down at Bull as he snored there beside her.

One night as Bull lay sleeping and Lizzie was slapping at mosquitoes, a woman on horseback rode up. She looked so pale in the moonlight Lizzie thought she was a white woman, but she saw that the horse belonged to her neighbor, old John Javilée. No mistaking that calico pony. The girl was sitting sidewise on a man's saddle, and she was wearing a shiny light dress and a Cape jasmine stuck back of her ear.

When she reached the gate she said: 'Mis' Lizzie, kin Ah come in a minute?'

Lizzie answered with the usual greeting to a visitor on horseback: 'Yas'm, sho' kin. Won't yo' git down?'

The girl slipped from the saddle and trailed up the walk, careless-like and slow. The lamplight was shining through the open door and Lizzie could see who she was. It was that bad one, Nita, who had made so much trouble five years ago that the white owner of the plantation had run her off the place. Now she was back again, wearing a silk dress, too. Lizzie's voice hardened. 'W'at yo' want comin' heah dis time er night?'

The girl didn't answer, but came slowly up the steps, dragging her pink dress after her. She almost stepped on Bull, who lay sprawled in the moonlight with his mouth open. She drew back with a cry, and Bull sat up, rubbing his eyes and staring at her.

But the girl's business was conducted inside the cabin with Lizzie. Women's business. Finally she climbed on her horse and rode away. When Lizzie came back to her chair, Bull began to ask questions.

Lizzie was not communicative, though bitter in her accusations against the girl. 'Jus' a low-down sport-woman,' she said. 'Dat's all Nita is.'

'Is she name Nita...? Dat's pretty.'

That made Lizzie angry. She told Bull all the bad things she had ever known about Nita, and she was in a position to know. Nita had fooled with the white clerk at the store; it had made Mr. Guy so angry he had sent her packing off the place. Everybody knew it. She was just plain worthless.

Afterwards she was sorry she had said so much. It was white folks' talk, and she knew Bull didn't care what Nita had been.

He lay awake a long time that night; and lying beyond the thin board partition, Lizzie couldn't sleep either.

Well, it wasn't a week before Bull and Nita were the talk of all the black men who sat along the store gallery at night, smoking their pipes and gazing at the moon as it hung like a red-hot stovelid above Cane River. It was crazy weather and Bull was a crazy man. He slept all day and never went into the field. And he was gone all night.

When Lizzie spoke to him he didn't answer; he just sat looking out across the cotton rows at the heat waves rising like steam from a pot. His eyes were bloodshot and his mouth hung open like a conjured man's. Nita had taught him to love her; he was possessed, as folks get possessed with devils.

You can't draw water from the well if you sit all day on the bucket, and it wasn't long before Mr. Guy's overseer rode over to see why Bull wasn't plowing in the cotton field. Lizzie said he was sick, and the white man rode away only half satisfied.

That week Nita came to live in Lizzie's cabin. The

black men on the store gallery didn't know what to make of it, and wouldn't have believed it if they hadn't seen Nita sitting there alongside of Lizzie Balize in the moonlight.

And it wasn't a month before trouble began. Nita was always wanting things, dresses and shoes and hats, and if Bull wouldn't give them to her, other men would. Lizzie had saved a little money; it was sewed in her mattress, and Nita found out about it. She begged Bull to get it for her. Lizzie finally gave in. In another week there were only some empty bottles and a sleazy red silk dress to show for it.

And daily Nita grew more restless. She would sit dreaming in the doorway, looking out along the cotton rows. 'What's de matter, honey?' Bull would say, following her gaze, and she would answer: 'Seems tuh me everything looks so pitiful-like out heah.'

'Yas, it do,' he would agree sullenly.

'It ain't never looked pitiful to yo' befo', Bull!' Lizzie said, bridling.

Sometimes there were quarrels in the light of the smoky lamp, and once, in defending Nita, Bull sent Lizzie sprawling on the floor, just as Aunt Dicey had said he would; and crying bitterly, his mother crept into bed without another word.

Lizzie was glad when Mr. Guy sent for her to come over at night and sit with his wife; she had been having malaria, and there was nobody to wait on her. It was easy and the pay was fair. Bull and Nita were left to themselves.

That was just what Nita wanted, and within a few days she had persuaded Bull to leave Cane River and go to the sawmill seven miles away to work for cash. Mr. Guy told Lizzie that she was a fool to let her son leave the share-land in the middle of the season. Bull and Lizzie had promised to take care of these acres for a year, but Lizzie could do nothing, and finally Mr. Guy had to take the land and they got nothing for their six months' work. Bull knew what it would mean if he left — but he went, and Nita and Lizzie were left alone in the cabin. Bull would come home Saturday night and leave before daylight Monday morning.

And it wasn't a week before Nita was slipping other men into Lizzie's cabin at night, while Lizzie was away. The black men gathered on the store gallery, wondered what Lizzie would do when she found it out; she had always been so strait-laced and respectable. Bull was a fool, tricked by a yellow woman. Aie yie! They had seen things happen before. But they felt ashamed for Lizzie, all ignorant of things. When she passed by on her way to Mr. Guy's that night she heard a smothered guffaw from the black men lolling on the gallery and guessed what it meant. She felt so low and broke-down she could hardly walk past. And all night — her last on duty — by the ill white woman, she brooded. She wanted to die. She had lived too long. Jesus and Bull had turned their backs on her. In her mind these two were somehow connected; she had worshiped them both.

As she was going home shortly after sunrise, her money in her apron pocket, Aunt Dicey called to her and told her what Nita had been doing. Lizzie didn't say anything. She just stood looking out over the cotton field. Finally, when the old woman stopped talking, Lizzie passed her hand over her scars and without a word went stumbling down the path between the furrows.

Nita lay across Lizzie's bed, asleep. There was a burnt hole in the sheet and a cigar butt on the floor beside the bed. The cabin reeked of smoke and perfume, but it was the cigar butt that roused Lizzie's anger. She sprang at the sleeping girl and shook her.

'Yo' low-down sport-woman!' she shouted. 'Ah'll tell Bull an' he'll kill yo'!'

Nita, only half awake, screamed: 'Tell 'im! ·Tell 'im, an' see ef I keer! An' see ef'n he'll believe yo'!'

Knowing which Bull would believe, Lizzie turned away baffled, and after a while began to clean the cabin. Hate hung like a curtain between them.

It was Wednesday, and Bull wouldn't be back till Saturday night. Lizzie wondered how she was going to stand it till he came, but Nita seemed to have no cares. The shadow of the well measured four o'clock as she walked along between the furrows to the gate and looked off down the road. By and by she came back and stood in the doorway, staring at Lizzie, who sat listless in a corner.

''Tain't no use in us sittin' heah fussin' till Sadday night,' Nita said lazily, 'so Ah'm goin' off. Ah'll be back befo' Bull gits heah. He done promise me ten dollars. We goin' tuh have us a time!'

There was a sound of buggy wheels in the road and a man whistled sharply. Nita turned and waved her hand, then looked back at Lizzie and said: 'Well — good-bye.'

Lizzie did not raise her head, but sat mumbling to herself.

She was alone in the cabin. The smoky lamp threw its ring of light on the white ceiling, but the corners of the room were dark. She was not doing anything. Her hands, usually busy, hung limp between her knees. Little white moths flew round the lamp; mosquitoes whined. It was airless, and from the trees by the door the odor of rotten figs came in. Sickly weather.

She was alone now; strangely enough she did not care. It was finished. But there was the misery in her head; thinking wouldn't let her rest. Studying out things was too much. She had tried praying but it did no good. God had forgotten her.

Hour after hour she sat listening to the night sounds; a cow lowing somewhere beyond the river, and a night bird repeating its mournful call. Then suddenly she shivered; from close by came the chitter of a screech-owl. The signs all against her. Just now a dirt-dauber's nest had fallen from the ceiling on her bed. That meant death. Aunt Dicey's dog had howled; and now this screech-owl. It was too much. Lizzie walked to the door. She could see two birds in the Chinaball tree, and shaking her apron at them she cried 'Shoo! Shoo!' There was a flutter of wings and they were gone — two streaks against the sky.

She looked out over the cotton stalks massed in the moonlight. Here and there a blossom hung pale against the night, and far off a rooster crowed — faint and clear. It was nearly midnight. Why couldn't she sleep? What was happening out there?

She went inside again, closed the door, and began, heavily, to undress. She lay down and looked up at the smoky lamp; she could hear the mosquitoes. Then at the sound of the gate and of fumbling on the porch she raised herself and called: 'Who dat?'

There was a muttering outside, something slumped against the door, and she knew it was Bull; but when she saw his face she reeled.

'Oh, Jesus ...'

His face was covered with whitish blisters. It was smallpox. Somehow she got him to bed — moaning and delirious; he kept asking over and over: 'Wha's Nita?'

She undressed him, on her own bed, and began putting wet cloths on him. His head was hot and his tongue thick. Somehow he had walked the seven miles back to the cabin. Until dawn she tried one homely remedy after another, but by the time the sun rose she knew that she must have a doctor.

As soon as she heard the first shouts in the field, of men plowing, she went outside and called. A black man left his mule, and she asked him to ask Mr. Guy at the store to telephone for the doctor to come; she had the money and could pay him. But the man must have guessed something, because it was not much after ten when Mr. Guy's overseer rode up. 'Bull!' he called. 'Answer me, you Goddamned nigger!' Lizzie went outside to explain: 'Bull's mighty sick.'

'Tell that nigger to put his head out of the window,' the overseer shouted, cursing her.

Bull was moaning and turning in bed, but Lizzie helped him to sit up, and the overseer looked through the window.

'Jesus Christ!' He drove spurs into the horse, and his face was pale as he galloped away.

Lizzie knew the word would travel up and down Cane River, as it had traveled years ago when a whole family had been wiped out. She had nursed them, and she knew how the thing terrified everybody, white and black. She wondered if the doctor would come. He did come, late that afternoon — not into the room, though. He left his buggy in the lane and walked up through the cotton field. He talked with her and finally came as far as the door. He left some ointment and quinine and told her what to do. She must make a smudge to keep out mosquitoes and flies and she must keep Bull from scratching himself. She went into the yard and cut down the clothesline and tied Bull's hands to the bed.

Bull kept moaning — the same thing over and over. 'Nita ... Nita ...' His tongue was black and swollen, and Lizzie would draw cool water from the well every half hour and give him little sips of it. She thought Aunt Dicey might come over to help, she had nursed her so many times; but at dusk she heard the rumble of wheels, and looking up she saw Aunt Dicey sitting on a trunk in a wagon while a half-grown boy whipped the slow old horse. She was moving, and didn't even look toward Lizzie's house.

Lizzie realized that nobody was going to help her. It was just Lizzie and Old Death wrestling for Bull. Well, she had a lot of strength left. Maybe she could pull him through.

He was worse in the night and kept moaning for ice. Early in the morning she started up the road, her money clutched in her hand. The black men on the store gallery dispersed as she came. Some ran down the road and some mounted and rode off. Before she got to the store the clerk came out and waved her back, calling: 'Don't you come here! Stop!'

She stood ankle-deep in the dust and said: 'Please,

suh, could yo' spare me a piece of ice? I kin pay for it —
wid cash money.'

He hesitated, then said: 'Stay where you are.'

Presently he came out and put some ice on the edge
of the gallery and asked: 'Anything else you want,
Lizzie?'

She named some groceries, and they were placed
alongside the ice, in an old sack. When the man had
retreated Lizzie picked up the package, laid the money
on the edge of the gallery, and went away. From down
the road as she looked back she saw the clerk pouring
disinfectant on the money.

Bull grew worse, and in his delirium was calling Nita.
As his strength ebbed his passion for her seemed to
grow. That night he never stopped moaning. Lizzie
longed to kill the girl. It was Nita. She had forced Bull
to go to the sawmill to work so he could buy silk dresses
for her. She had fooled him, and now when he was
brought low, she was gone.

By Saturday Lizzie knew Bull was going to die.

'Oh, Gawd, Oh, Jesus, lissen,' she prayed. 'Jus' a
minute, Jesus . . . jus' a minute. Oh, Jesus . . . lemme
git Nita for 'im . . . lemme git 'er, so he can die easy.'

A buggy rattled by in the road. Was it the doctor?
It was the middle of the night. Had Jesus heard her
prayer and sent Nita back? She went outside. The
buggy had stopped and Nita was climbing out. She
swayed drunkenly between the cotton rows, her silk

dress trailing out behind her. Lizzie went to meet her. There was some good in the woman, then. She had come back to nurse Bull.

'Oh, Nita,' she said, 'yo' is jus' in time.'

Nita stood swaying there in the moonlight. 'What yo' mean, I is jus' in time? Is Bull inside?' And she laughed a little defiantly.

She did not know then what Bull had. In some strange way Nita was the only person that didn't know. Lizzie, sick with weariness, could not think it out.

'Wha — wha — is 'e sick? Wha's matter wid 'em?' Nita stopped beside a yellow rosebush. 'Is 'e got some catchin' sickness?'

They stepped over the threshold. Bull lay on his back, his breath coming in gasps. The odor of smallpox filled the room, but a card stuck against the lamp shaded the bed. Nita went close, staggering a little, to look. 'Bull . . .' she said, 'it's me, honey . . . It's yo' Nita.'

Lizzie turned the lamp so it shone full on his face. For a moment Nita gazed transfixed, then sprang to the door and with a bound was down the walk. But Lizzie was after her, running with her head forward like an animal. She caught her as she was fumbling with the gate and grabbed her round the waist, and without a word the two women wrestled. But the thin young mulatto was no match for the negro woman; together they fell to the ground — Lizzie's fingers closing around Nita's throat, pressing harder.

When the other had stopped struggling, Lizzie carried her into the house, untied Bull's wrists, and with the cord tied Nita down beside him. She stood holding the oil lamp and looking at them as they lay there. Nita was regaining her senses, moaning now and turning her head from side to side. She was like a crazy woman when she realized what had happened. Then she quieted down, cried, prayed, and begged Lizzie to let her up, promising to stay and nurse Bull, to work for Lizzie — anything. But Lizzie was deaf to her. She did the work, nursed Bull and fed Nita — even lengthened the rope so the girl could sit on the edge of the bed.

She had a few dollars left, and every second day she went to the store to get groceries and ice, and walked home again. Folks gave her a wide berth. On the ninth day she called to the clerk that Bull was dead and that he'd better tell Mr. Guy to send men to bury him.

They came that afternoon and dug a grave near the front steps in Lizzie's little flower-garden. They were old men, scarred with smallpox, and were not afraid. When they had dug the hole they went inside and helped Lizzie put Bull's body in the rough pine box they had brought. It was then they saw Nita lying in Lizzie's bed, covered with white sores. No one knew she had come back.

Lizzie nursed her as she had nursed Bull and she got better, but her face was covered with red scars.

One day she was able to sit up, and Lizzie pulled a

chair out on the narrow gallery for her, so she could look past the flower-garden, past the cotton field to the road where folks were going by. Nita had asked for a mirror, so Lizzie left her while she went to the store to get it. It would cost a dollar.

# CHAPTER XX

THE first breeze of Autumn swept down upon the plantation, rustling the leaves and causing a great fluttering among the bluejays in the China trees. There was a tang in the air and Joel was impelled to run about, to stretch his arms, to sing without understanding why. The fields were white with cotton, and in the broad expanse he could see groups of negroes with their long white sacks trailing on the ground behind them, like ladies with long dresses — cotton-pickers working from dawn until dusk.

All day long the wagons went toward the gin, large fluffy loads of white, with small boys in blue overalls perched high on top, and the mules bending their necks to the load. All day long the cries for the ferry were heard, as wagons rumbled down to the flatboat. Joel watched the reflections of the wagons in the water as the boat was propelled across the river by a rope which stretched from bank to bank.

In the plantation commissary the clerk was laying out his winter supplies — gay shirts for the men, new overalls, gaudy bandanna handkerchiefs, harness, new and shining saddles, lanterns, gay-colored dishes, coffee-pots; the shelves were piled with bolts of colored cloth, vivid green crying out against turkey red, purple vying with orange; and there were sweaters, more gaudy than warm, filling one whole counter in the center of the store. The white man was making ready the yearly temptation for the black man's cotton money. Old accounts were squared up, new accounts were opened.

Joel was ten years old and large for his age. He looked out upon his world with clear blue eyes. This year, for the first time, he began to look about him, noticing the entities which made up his familiar life. Until now he had accepted it all, but now he was beginning to ask questions.

He saw the difference between yesterday and today, for after yesterday's depression and 'hard times' the negroes were rich folks now. Guitars tinkled on the river bank in the evening and songs re-echoed in the moonlight. Troubles and poverty were forgotten; the negroes were spending now. It was impossible to get a negro to do anything. A dollar was as nothing. He had his cash in hand and was stepping high.

Miss Adelaide, standing beside the four-post bed as she examined the laundry with Famie, sighed as she listened to the cook's complaints: Yesterday Mug was the picture of health and sang baptizing songs as she cooked, but last night Henry-Jack, her husband, sold his cotton, and today Mug moaned and said that she was ready to die with pain. She had a misery in her head, her stomach ached, she was a sick woman, she must go and see the doctor in town, otherwise she would never see the old year out.

Miss Adelaide listened, sighed, laughed, threw up her hands, and accepted the inevitable. 'Go on, Mug,' she said. 'Have your good time and come on back. I'll manage with Aunt Dicey until you finish spending your money.' Joel and his mother exchanged a smile but said nothing.

And in the commissary Henry-Jack was telling Mr. Guy that he had a rich brother in Texas that he hadn't seen in fourteen years. He wanted to go and pay him a visit.

The planter shrugged his shoulders. 'Go ahead, Henry-Jack, but don't come to me in a week and say that you haven't got a cent and that you've just got to have five dollars.'

Joel and Famie, standing beside the counter, heard the conversation as they purchased cornmeal and salt meat, and Famie said in an undertone: 'Niggers is neahly all like that. Let 'em go, Ah say, an' they'll come whin'lin' home befo' Chris'mas. Yo'll see. Ah've seen it befo' an' Ah knows.'

When they came out of the commissary Joel saw that Cane River was a deeper blue, and dead trees reflected themselves like white skeletons in the clear water. The sky was banked high with fleecy clouds; herons flew low over the fields, and a few yellow leaves drifted through the sunlit air.

The mother and her son hurried home to help Numa in the cotton field.

Numa was alone in the vast sea of cotton. His thin shoulders were bent under the weight of the heavy sack that dragged behind him. His hands were cold and his forehead was burning, and he staggered as he stood erect to ease his aching back. When he looked toward the house he saw Famie and Joel coming into the field, their empty sacks slung over their shoulders. He waved his arm and they called to him.

There was a large empty cotton-basket at the end of the row and he went toward it to lighten his load. When Famie and Joel came near they saw that he had filled the basket and was kneeling, leaning upon it. He did not lift his head as they approached, and when they came close they saw that blood was flowing from his mouth and that the cotton in the basket was dyed red.

Someway, between them, they carried him home and put him on the bed. Famie's cries had attracted half a dozen of the nearer cotton-pickers, and now, black faces peered in at the door. Henry Tyler had abandoned his sack in the field and run to the commissary to get help.

Numa lay fighting for breath, his eyes staring up at the ceiling where a mud-dauber was putting a paralyzed spider into a living tomb of damp clay. His hands picked at the coverlet, and he made an effort to speak.

Famie, kneeling beside the bed, spoke softly to him: 'Please don' try to talk, Numa, please...' And Joel stood staring at him with frightened blue eyes. But Numa knew that death was upon him, knew he must speak now or he would never speak. There was something that he must tell her before the priest came across the river in his little boat...

He made an effort and said: 'Clock.'

She did not understand him. 'Please, Numa...' she pleaded.

But he said again: 'Bring me the clock...'

Joel understood, and looked from his mother to the timepiece on the mantel.

'He's sick; he don' know what he's sayin'...'

But Numa's gesture was emphatic: 'Heah... bring it heah.'

A black woman spoke from the doorway: 'He got somethin' hid in theah. He tryin' tuh give it tuh yo'.'

Joel took the clock down from the mantel; it was

heavier than he anticipated and he stumbled. The clock fell over on the bed with a jangling of gong and springs. Numa's finger pointed to the bottom of the clock-case and the boy saw that a piece of wood had been put there. His small white fingers tugged, and the thin piece of wood came out. Ten twenty-dollar bills — two hundred dollars — lay scattered on the bed.

Numa's fingers gathered them up. He put them in Joel's hand and said: 'They belongs to yo'...' And to Famie he said: 'Ah lied to yo', Famie ... please ...'

Her gaze went from his pallid face to the crucifix which hung on the wall. She remembered the day he had sworn that it was another and not he who had told the sheriff of the red-haired man's hiding-place. For a moment she felt all the old bitterness. It was Numa, her husband, who had betrayed her. And it was the blood money of the reward that Joel now held in his hand. It was all a lie ...

But as she stood looking down at the face of the dying man another thought came. She knew now, as she understood the eternal fear in his eyes, that his misery had been greater than her own. She had Joel, but Numa had nothing. He had never had anything. And now he was dying.

She fell upon her knees beside the bed. 'Ah know, Numa, an' Ah don' care. It's past an' gone an' forgot. Ah swear, Numa.' She pressed her lips against his forehead.

He could not feel her lips, for he was numb, but in the darkness that gathered around him he could see her face and he knew that she had forgiven him. He sighed, and a thin stream of blood ran from the corner of his mouth upon the white pillow. As Famie wiped it away, she knew that he was dead.

His eyes were closed and he no longer breathed, but as she stared at him two large tears, white with salt, pushed out from under his closed eyelids and ran slowly down his brown cheeks.

Neighbors, relatives, and friends came flocking to Numa's funeral and remained to help pick the cotton. Famie saw them as though she were dreaming: brown hands in the white cotton, shoulders bearing the heavy baskets to the waiting wagons, strangers looking at her, offering her kind words, telling her that everything was going to be all right. There were many people to be fed, and she crouched over the fireplace for the greater part of each day, working mechanically. The coffee-pot seldom left the hearth. Joel remained away from the house all day, embarrassed as curious glances were directed at his white skin and blue eyes.

When the crop was all gathered the people went away, leaving Famie and Joel alone again, and the quiet seemed like heaven. The cotton crop was the best that Numa had ever made; even when all outstanding bills were paid, and money set aside for the taxes, there was enough for his funeral and sixty dollars left to put away for the future.

Numa's mother and Famie were putting fresh flowers on his grave, and removing the dead flowers which remained from the funeral two weeks before. The freshly turned earth was already pressed down by the rain, and small flecks of mud discolored the white headstone. The inscription read:

*Numa Lacour*
*Beloved husband of*
*Euphemie Vidal Lacour,*
*Born, May 13, 1886*
*Died, September 4, 1915.*
*Age 29 years*
*May he rest in peace*

The old woman sat on the ground, and tears ran down her cheeks. Famie stood beside her, thin in her black dress, her shoulders stooped; she was only twenty-six years old, but she looked forty. Youth was gone, and already there were streaks of gray in her dark hair.

Old Madame Lacour was thinking of the boy who lay buried there: he had been so good, she thought, and life had been so cruel to him; and now he was dead and buried and would soon be forgotten. Who would re-

member him? Who would know that he had lived and
worked and suffered? Famie would remember for a
while and she, his mother, but who else? In time they
would all be gone and there would be no one left. Most
men, she thought, leave children behind them, and
children made a man immortal, a man lived on in them;
but Numa had left nothing, only a mound of earth and
a headstone already discolored with mud. The old
woman wanted to tell Famie her thoughts, but she was
too tired, and talking was too hard.

The younger woman helped old Madame Lacour to
her feet and they turned toward the cemetery gate.
The old woman was mumbling to herself.

'What's that yo're sayin', *Nainaine?*' Famie asked.

'The' ain't no meanin' to it,' Numa's mother said.
'Maybe it's a sin to say it, but Ah can' help it. The'
ain't no understandin' it. It all seem so senseless.'

Famie went about her tasks with but one thought in
her mind: Joel. He was everything she had, and he was
enough. When he was away at school, he seemed almost as near as when he lay sleeping beside her in the
old four-post bed from which the red tester-cloth hung
in tatters.

It was impossible for Famie to think of Joel as anything but a child. In the afternoons she would walk far
along the lane which led toward the flatboat that
brought him back from school, waiting for him, and

hand and hand they would go home together. She prepared little tidbits that she knew he would like, stinting
herself gladly for his sake. It was pride that made her
sit up nearly all night making his clothes, shirts, and
trousers, with the finest of buttonholes and made from
the best material that the store at Yucca afforded.

Her relatives were tolerant, shaking their heads and
calling her foolish, but she had been like that always,
they said. They almost forgot her, although her cottage was not far from her neighbor — a scant quarter
mile through the cotton field — a field that Famie
rented out, nowadays, to old John Javilée, never ques-
tioning his erratic payments so long as there was enough
for Joel to have the things he needed.

She loved his body, so white and so slim. He was
whiter than any of the other children. He was like a red-
haired Spaniard, with his large blue eyes and his thin,
clean-cut profile. It was her greatest pleasure that he be
kept neat and clean. In the winter, when he complained
because the water was too cold, Famie would carry
bucket after bucket of water up the river bank into the
cabin, and would put all the kettles and pots into the
fireplace at once. She would kneel beside the hearth,
pouring first hot water, then cold, into a zinc tub and
the blue-ringed washbowl, until the water was as Joel
desired it. Then he would undress and stand before her,
slim and shivering, despite the fire's warmth, while she
bathed him. She lingered over him, drying him in an

old sheet, nursing his small body, caressing him, kissing his knees, his feet. Sleepily he would lie in her arms, his fingers on her face, as she sat beside the dying fire, great boy that he was, eleven years old. Already he was tolerant with her, sensing her light-headedness, letting her make herself happy by caressing him.

When he was away she pictured these homely scenes, living them over and over, in every detail. The blue-ringed washbowl was sacred. She even liked the ring of moisture left by the bowl on the wide boards of the floor.

When Joel was twelve there was a fine down on his upper lip. Sometimes he spoke in a deep voice, almost like a man, but at other times his quavering tones were those of a small boy. But Famie never seemed to notice. He was her baby and she still bathed him every night, but by tacit agreement these babyings went on behind closed doors. At night she would draw back the covers and look at his white body against the sheets, leaning down to kiss him, then drawing back for fear of waking him. At these times she felt a sort of ecstasy, a desire to sing, to stretch her arms, to dance. Instead she would open the door and slip out into the moonlight. One night old Javilée saw her lying on the river bank, crooning to herself, her arms uplifted toward the moon. She did not even know that he had passed near her.

Now that Joel was older he would go out in the evenings to play with the other boys on the river bank, coming home down the dusty road in the moonlight to the light which glimmered in Famie's cottage. She would be waiting for him always, with a glass of milk or a sweet cake.

At thirteen Joel began wearing a flower behind his ear, as other mulattoes did — the flower that amused the white folks and the negroes tolerated.

A man from New Orleans who visited Mr. Guy over at Yucca once said that the mulattoes with gardenias behind their ears reminded him of the Street of the Dancing Boys in Bombay, but Mr. Guy, who had never heard of the Street of the Dancing Boys, did not understand him. It was this white man who had talked to Joel one evening on the river bank — astonished when he heard from the boy's own lips that he was of mixed blood.

'You could pass for white anywhere,' he said.

Famie felt exultation when Joel repeated this to her. 'Of co'se! Of co'se you could,' she said. 'You *is* white, son.'

Joel had never asked who his father was and Famie had never told him, but from hints heard from his cousins he had divined something of the truth; and from their air of respect he knew that it was nothing of which to be ashamed.

It was the white man at Yucca who gave Joel city newspapers, and it was then, for the first time, that the boy saw pictures of a city with office buildings and street-cars and hundreds of automobiles.

That night Joel sat looking at the papers by the yellow light of the kerosene lamp; his face was intent as he examined each picture again and again, asking questions which Famie could not answer.

'What Ah know about it?' she said as she looked fondly at him. The lamplight glittered on her poised needle, for she was mending a torn shirt for him. 'Ah've never been mo' than twenty miles from Isle Brevelle in my whole life.'

Joel gazed straight ahead, and his eyes were shining. 'Ah'm goin' someday, Mama, seems like Ah've jus' got to go.'

His words frightened her, and yet she knew that this moment was inevitable; deep in her consciousness she had always known that this time must come. She knew that some day Joel must go out into that unknown white world which lay beyond her knowledge or conjecture. Until this moment that time had seemed far away, but now the words were spoken. It seemed to her that somewhere in the distance she heard a bell tolling.

'Not yet, Joel,' she said, trying to keep her voice steady. 'Wait until yo're a man, son. Time enough then.'

'Ah'm ole enough,' he said, 'an' Ah'm tired a-waitin'.'

The hard quality in his tone was so like the remembered voice of the red-haired man that Famie quivered in her chair. She knew that she could never hold out against his determination. She had an almost forgotten cousin in Chicago. Should she send him there — to school, perhaps? But somehow the time for departure must be put off; she could not bear to see him go. Not yet.

Joel was becoming secretive. He no longer told his mother of his nightly games with the other children, nor did he speak of school. He went out in the evenings nowadays and came home quietly, slipping into bed without coming into his mother's room to kiss her goodnight; and when she attempted to caress him he put her aside.

'Ah'm too big for that, Mama,' he said.

Famie's face gave no sign of the hurt she felt, but she left the room without a word.

Now she found herself watching him, wondering what he thought about as he sat dreaming in the doorway, looking out along the cotton rows. When he went out into the summer night she waited jealously for his return, lying awake in her room, staring into the dark.

Cotton-picking was over and the gin was silent once more. Only small patches of sugar cane were green in the empty fields. Many of the mulattoes grew a small plot of cane for molasses-making, using a horse-driven press for extracting the sweet juice from the *bagasse* and boiling the juice, following the old recipes which their grandfathers had used.

On the river bank, near the spot where the flatboat was moored, there was an acre of sugar cane standing on Famie's land; John Javilée had planted it there, and it stood now a sharp green rectangle against blue of river and brown of field. Soon it would be cut.

As Famie was coming home from the commissary one sunlit afternoon, she saw the flatboat crossing the river, and the bright dresses of the little girls were reflected in the water; probably ten or more children were coming home from school, their bodies swaying rhythmically as they pulled in unison on the cable. She recognized Joel's blue shirt, and she lingered in the road, waiting for him to see her. As the boat approached the bank the tall sugar cane hid the group from sight, but presently she saw the children coming through the field. Boys and girls came together, shouting messages to others who were going the other way by the river path. Joel, she knew, would pass near her on the trail which led toward home. Famie seated herself at the edge of the deep ditch and waited. She was tired from a long day of ironing, and as she rested she watched five black buzzards sailing high in the golden air. How gracefully they sailed and swooped as they circled lower! Strange to think that such grace belonged to these scavengers; strange, too, to think that they were so lovely against the clouds when they were so ugly as they came close — those buzzards with their blood-red, bald heads and their shining, funereal feathers — but high in the air they were like black angels flying . . .

She raised her head and looked along the path. It was empty; the other children had gone, but Joel had not yet emerged from the patch of sugar cane. Perhaps he had stopped to watch a snake or small animal. She rose and walked slowly through the furrows toward the cane patch.

The cane looked like a solid wall as she approached; she could not see more than three or four feet into its denseness. Joel was nowhere in sight, but as she came close to the green barrier she stopped short in surprise. A girl's hat lay forgotten on the ground, a gay white hat with a bow of red ribbon.

Famie stood still in the furrow, looking down at the hat, then she called sharply: 'Joel!'

There was a rustling in the cane, and presently the boy appeared between the stalks, his hair tousled, his face red. When he saw her standing there before him, his cold blue eyes flashed with anger.

'What yo' want?' he said, and then with mounting anger he shouted: 'What yo' followin' me fo'? Why can't yo' lemme alone?'

She was afraid for a moment that he would strike her, as he stood before her with clenched fists.

She did not answer, but somewhere close at hand she could hear the rustling cane, and she knew that the girl was running away.

Famie turned and went draggingly home through the field alone.

She could not sleep that night but lay thinking; her thoughts went back and forth like a squirrel in a cage, endlessly moving, getting nowhere. Mr. Guy had said: 'If my own son ran after nigger women I'd send him off, just as I'm sending you.' And then she remembered the clerk's whining answer. How long ago that seemed! But now it was Joel, her son. Impossible, but it was true. She couldn't think it out, but one thing was certain: Joel must go away, and he must go at once. She couldn't let him stay and become enmeshed in the life around him. Henry Tyler said that he was 'stuck like a fly in molasses,' and Numa had died in his struggle with the land, but Joel must have a chance, somewhere. This incident today had shown Famie that the time had come, and that she must let him go.

She rose from the bed, lighted a lamp, and took the money from the clock. There was still two hundred dollars left, and it was enough. She could sell something, borrow money somewhere. The money that she held in her hand could take him away and keep him for three or four months, perhaps; after that she must find more. She sat down and wrote the cousin in Chicago, asking that Joel be allowed to come for a visit, and that, if she could pay his board, he be allowed to go to school for a time.

A week later she went with him to the flag-station on the railroad, six miles away down an unfamiliar road. The little village was called Cypress, the station was lighted with smoking kerosene lamps, and trains stopped only on signal.

Joel was very quiet, wearing his best black suit, and carrying a new and shiny suitcase which he had bought from the plantation store for a dollar and a half. There were tears in his eyes when he kissed her good-bye, but Famie smiled at him. 'A little while,' she kept repeating to herself. 'Ah'll see him again in a little while.'

When they saw the headlight of the engine in the dark, John Javilée lighted a piece of paper which he had rolled and dipped into oil before leaving home. The improvised torch flared as the old man waved it up and down; far off they heard the engine whistle in reply.

The train came puffing in and Joel climbed on board hastily, looking back only once as the train began to move again. When the lights had faded out and the train was gone into the darkness, Famie went back to Javilée's wagon and climbed in, bright-eyed and silent. An idea had come to her by which she thought she could make money to send to Joel. The moon rose round and red as they rode home down the lane between two cotton fields.

# CHAPTER XXI

THE more I see of this Cane River country the stranger it seems to me,' said Harry Smith, as he and Mr. Guy sat on the commissary gallery late one afternoon. It was just sunset, and the negroes were bringing the mules in from the fields. A fine haze of dust hung in the air above the road. The two men sat in hide-bottomed chairs, tilted back against the posts which supported the roof, and a small negro boy was shining Mr. Randolph's boots.

'What's puzzling you now?' asked Mr. Guy.

The two men had become friends, and the Smiths came for visits several times each year.

'I was wondering what you meant when you said that this woman Famie Lacour was losing caste with the other mulattoes.'

'Did I say that? Oh, yes, I meant that her kin people

resented her selling the old furniture out of her house to Flossie and Adelaide. As a matter of fact, Harry, you and I ought to resent it, for what our wives want with all that old stuff is more than I can see. I wouldn't have given her ten dollars for everything she had in her house.'

'Flossie is smarter about that sort of business than you'd think,' said Smith. 'She opened my eyes when she sold two little tables for a hundred and fifty dollars. I was flabbergasted. She bought them for two dollars up here and had them refinished in New Orleans. I heard the dealer offer that price myself. Sheraton, he said, two very rare pieces. Anyway, it's Flossie's own money, and she can do as she likes with it. And it keeps her busy and interested in something. She's a born trader, always buying something somewhere. But you were telling me about this Famie Lacour getting in wrong with her relatives. What did you mean?'

Guy Randolph yawned and gave the small negro boy two nickels: 'Run along, son, Mr. Smith doesn't want a shine.' After the boy was out of earshot, he continued: 'I don't like to talk before them; you never know how much they understand and repeat.'

'Yes, I suppose so.'

'About Famie Lacour, it's a long story, but here it is in a word or two. She belongs to the "high-up" mulattoes — I mean that she is a descendant of the original Vidal family — and in consequence she holds her head high . . .'

'Wait a minute, Guy, what do you mean by the original Vidal family?'

'Well, sometime about 1760 or thereabouts, two brothers came from France. Rich men, both of them, and they had a land grant on Red River, here in north-western Louisiana. One of them stopped off in New Orleans and picked up a woman at the quadroon balls there, and he brought her up here.'

'Yes, I've read about those quadroon balls; they must have been quite an institution.'

'Yes. You've got to remember that Louisiana was a French colony at that time and the French had no race prejudices, and white women were scarce in Louisiana. Fathers hired mulatto mistresses for their sons — something to keep them quiet until they married. Well, anyway, this Frenchman, Vidal, brought a young quadroon girl to this wilderness — it was a wilderness then — and settled right here where Yucca Plantation is today. He was wealthy and he was thrifty, and he acquired about eighteen miles of land on Red River ... all this country around here, in fact. And then he died and left his property to his "free-mulatto children" and to his wife.'

'Did he actually marry this girl?'

'No, he couldn't have done that. You can't marry negroes in Louisiana. But it amounted to the same thing. He left his property to his children, and they grew up and married in turn. They brought in their wives from New Orleans or Opelousas. It must have been an interesting group, here on the river. I mean that the first generation produced the one they call *Grandpère* Augustin. You've seen his portrait at his granddaughter's house. Augustin seems to have been the father of the flock, a sort of patriarch. He was born in 1768 and he lived until just before the Civil War. That portrait of him was painted when he was nearly seventy years old, and it amuses me because his dignity was so great. But he must have been a fine old fellow. He divided his property among his children, and they had French architects come and build houses. Augustin had more than a hundred nigger slaves.'

'What sort of relations did he have with white people?'

'Pretty friendly, from all I can gather,' said Mr. Guy. 'He was rich, and he was proud, and he was independent. And distances were so great in those days that no one interfered with him. He was a sort of king, I gather, among his relatives.'

'Odd that he had his portrait painted,' said the other.

'No, I don't think so. White planters had their portraits made, and painters traveled around in those days. And Augustin was proud that he had given the first Catholic church in the community. But all this is getting tiresome to you — I'll cut it short. Sometime just before the Civil War, Red River changed its course and left this part behind ... I mean that the river cut through into a new bed and left about sixty miles of meandering stream; that's what we call Cane River to-day. The mulattoes were left here...their means of transportation was gone. Steamboats couldn't get through the shallow water that remained.

'Then came the war, and the mulatto slave-owners suffered just as the white slave-owners did. Old Augustin was dead, and there was no leader among them. The land was divided again and again. My grandfather acquired this plantation, right in the middle of the mulatto holdings.

'Then they became poorer and poorer. All they had was land, and they could make a living, but that was about all. Then strange families moved in. The mulattoes resented that, and kept to themselves. They began marrying their cousins. The whole settlement is related now...And of course, all this inbreeding began to have its results. It's strange, Harry, but there's little degeneracy among them...I mean physical degeneracy as well as mental. There are a few idiots, of course, but that's about all. They're a good race of people. They're gentle and kindly, but all the shrewdness is drained out of them. They've retained a sort of gentleness, a sort of decency...You've seen lots of white Louisiana families like that, too, of course...I mean that they can't cope with life. They're defeated. And, of course, like all other farmers, they've become poor.

'Their pride, and their land and their few possessions

are all they have left ... To get back to this girl **Famie:**
She is a direct descendant of old Augustin, and she mar-
ried her cousin, also a direct descendant of the old fellow.
But she had a child by a white man.'

'That was pretty bad, hanh?'

'No, not so bad. It was better than having an illegiti-
mate child by another mulatto. That's a sort of tacit
agreement among mulattoes. It's almost as though they
were scheming to make the race lighter. Now, if she
had had a child by a black man ... well, that would have
been the unforgivable sin. She would have been an out-
cast.'

'Well, then how is she losing caste?'

'Just this. She was obsessed about this white child of
hers. I used to see her here, watching my children. She
noticed what they said, what they ate, what they wore
... and then her child did the same thing. Of course she
spoiled him to death. He was a handsome little fellow,
but mean. And the meaner he was to her, the better
she was to him ... Well, now he's gone.'

'You mean he's left her?'

'No, she sent him away. He's probably going to
school somewhere. She's selling everything she has to
keep him there.'

'Well, I don't see ...'

'It's their pride, man! She had some of the original
Vidal furniture. That grandfather's clock, for instance,
belonged to *Grandpère* Augustin. She sold it for five

dollars. She had some of his silver, too. Your wife bought that.'

'You mean that the mulattoes resent a white person owning their things?'

'I suppose that's as near as I can come to explaining what I mean,' said Mr. Guy, 'but someway the other mulattoes feel that she's selling them out. Look, I'll go further. Some of these days she'll come to me and offer to sell a few acres of her land, and I'll buy it cheap. Naturally, I want it; it adjoins Yucca. But every mulatto in the neighborhood will resent it; they'll want to acquire it for themselves. But they'll not have the money. They'll want to pay for it on time, but she'll want cash, and I'm the only person here who has cash and who wants the land.

'They'll accuse me of robbing her, of buying the land for one quarter of its value. That's ridiculous. I'll make an offer, and she'll accept it. Watch, and you'll see. I'll give her four or five years, not longer.'

'And then what will happen to her?'

'Well, I don't know exactly. Everything and nothing. She'll be a betrayer, an outsider. If she's lucky, she'll die, or go away; if she's unlucky, she'll stay here and take the slights of her friends and neighbors...'

'Somebody ought to write a book about this country.'

'Oh, writers!' Guy Randolph's tone was scornful. 'When Paul was alive, some of his writing friends came here, and they talked me to death. Such a bunch of idiots you never saw. They were divided into two classes: one saw everything as symbolical — whatever they meant by that, I don't know — and found everything quaint: they saw the surface, and it was just as picturesque as hell. They talked about folklore and all that sort of bunk. The other group talked about the plight of the share-croppers. God! As though I wouldn't get rid of the share-croppers if I could. It's a rotten system, but what am I going to do about it? I've tried to work the men as day laborers, but I can't pay them more than a dollar a day — when they work — and they can't live on it. And they get poorer and poorer. And they don't like it, anyway. They leave me if I don't let them have land on shares . . . I'm damned if I see any way out of it all. I'm sick of the whole business.'

The other man laughed: 'Hell, Guy, you couldn't be pried loose from Yucca with a crow-bar.'

'That's right. I belong here, and the land belongs to me. I couldn't live anywhere else. Adelaide feels the same way, I suppose. And even Paul came home to die.'

'I can never think of you two as brothers, someway. You were as different as night and day.'

'Paul stayed away too long, and he got full of Yankee notions,' said Mr. Guy. 'We didn't talk the same language any more. He thought that we exploited the niggers . . . all that sort of bunk. We'd argue for hours on end. He said some pretty sensible things, too, sometimes. But he couldn't find a solution any more than I can.'

'There's the supper bell.'

The two men rose and went through the gate into the flower-garden. It was dusk and the stars were beginning to show in the clear sky, yellow lamplight shone from the open doors and windows of the big-house; Miss Adelaide and Flossie were waiting on the gallery, their light summer dresses pale in the gathering darkness.

'Oh, *there* you are!' cried Flossie; 'and it's high time, too. Adelaide and I have been waiting for *hours*. I wonder what you men find to talk about all the time. Something boring, I'm sure. Crops and things like that. Don't you think so, Adelaide? We've been waiting to show you the silver we got from that mulatto woman to-day. My dear, it's *beautiful*. Adelaide and I have been polishing and *polishing*. Look at it, all spread out on the table. It's wonderful, really it is. Only, of course, nothing is complete. Eleven tablespoons ... but *look* at them! See how *heavy* they are, and so *plain* and lovely and all the forks, too. They were so *black* they looked like *iron*. And eighteen *teaspoons*, and a silver soup-tureen. We carried them home ourselves. It was such a *bargain*.'

'What did you pay for all that trash?' asked Mr. Guy, laughing.

'*Trash?*' Flossie screamed. 'Oh, Adelaide, listen to him. *Trash?* Well, I'll tell you this, Guy Randolph, there's about a hundred dollars' worth of silver there, and we got it for ten dollars. Trash, the *idea!* And we could have bought it for less than that, only I got *ashamed.* We had just stripped her house *clean,* beds and chairs and sideboard and *everything,* for a dollar or two dollars a piece — of course, I've got to ship it all to New Orleans and the freight will be more than I paid for it, but just the same ——'

'Supper gettin' cole...' said Mug from the doorway.

'Oh, of *course* it is, how inconsiderate of me to keep you all standing here... Adelaide, why didn't you tell me, I'm so *sorry*... Oh, biscuits and fried *chicken.* My dear, if I keep on eating all this good food, I'll be as big as a *house.* Oh, darling Adelaide, I just love staying with you here at Yucca. It's all so *peaceful.* Yes, I'll take two and butter them while they're hot. Harry will tell you that I love this place better than home. I get ashamed of myself, but it's the *truth.* In New Orleans I just tell everybody how lucky Adelaide is, living in peace and quiet on the old plantation.'

~~~~~~~~~~~~~~~~~~~~~~~~~~~~~~~~~~~~~~~~~~~~~~~~~~~

# PART FOUR

## *BLACK AND WHITE*

~~~~~~~~~~~~~~~~~~~~~~~~~~~~~~~~~~~~~~~~~~~~~~~~~~~

# CHAPTER XXII

IT WAS summer again.

From every bush and tree the mocking-birds were singing as Famie went up the lane that led along the river bank to the big-house at Yucca. The chorus swept higher and higher in the sunlight, mocking-birds, mostly, and the high sweet trilling of a wren, a bird invisible in a glowing pomegranate bush. The plantation was astir. Mules and negroes in the fields, men down on the river bank repairing the flatboat, singing as they worked. Famie made a circuit of the flower-garden and went around to the back of the house. A dozen or more little negro boys and girls were picking figs, with which the trees were loaded. Famie saw them perched in the trees, their mouths smeared with ripe figs, and their faded blue overalls making splotches of color where the sun came in between the bending branches. The negro yardman was going about among the trees giving advice and admonition. She could not hear the words, but the tone told her that he was finding fault with the fig-pickers. Their voices, irresponsible and shrill, came thinly through the golden air and they continued blithely to eat, putting almost as many figs into their mouths as they did into the buckets. No matter, there are figs enough for all, more than enough. Beneath the trees chickens had gathered, picking up the fruit as it fell, with much fluttering and quarreling among them. The Rhode Island Reds were the most aggressive, pushing aside the smaller fowls with sweeping and fluttering of tawny wings.

One hen with a topknot held her own valiantly, returning peck for peck and even adding a few for good measure. Childishly pleased, Famie stopped to look and smile: 'Law, chicken!' she said aloud.

The little negroes in the trees paid no attention to the hen's dignity, but pelted her with ripe figs. After the first agonized squawking she turned the missiles to account, and carried a purple fig off into the high grass under the farther trees.

Famie passed on and approached the house. The back gallery, a long brick-paved loggia flush with the ground, had been turned into a temporary kitchen. Charcoal furnaces were burning, and upon these large kettles of figs were simmering. Mr. Guy's wife was making preserves. She did this as she did everything else — with dash. Half a dozen kettles boiled at once over slow fires, and Miss Adelaide, her skirts caught up, went from kettle to kettle, stirring with a large iron spoon. Upon a table a hundred glass jars stood, shining and clean, with their screw-tops in a heap beside them. Mr. Guy's mother, wearing a white wrapper, was sitting in the shade, peeling purple figs into a yellow bowl. Sunlight shining through leaves made dappled shadows upon her white hair, and as she worked she sang a little song, thin and wavering, and her song seemed to become a part of the great chorus of sound that was everywhere today.

Famie came closer: 'Good-mawnin', Miz Adelaide!'

The mistress of the house smiled: 'Well, well, Famie, I'm glad to see you. It's been months. I've hardly talked to you since Joel went away. I was sorry about that, for I know you miss him. Looks like we have more trouble than our share, here on Yucca, sometimes . . .' Her voice trailed off vaguely, and she began stirring one of the kettles. 'Sit down, Famie, you look tired. I'll get Mug to give you a cup of coffee.'

Inside the kitchen, Mug, the fat black cook, snorted: 'Humph! Givin' coffee to them mulattoes, same as if they wuz white folks!' she said under her breath.

Miss Adelaide laughed. 'All right, Mug, fuss as much as you like, but hurry up with the coffee.'

Mollified, Mug laughed: 'Law, Miz Famie knows

what it is to a 'ooman to be interrup' in de midst of bakin' a cake.'

'Please don' take no trouble...' Famie was beginning, but Miss Adelaide was no longer within hearing distance, having gone out to the fig trees to admonish the fig-pickers to renewed activity.

It was half an hour before Famie was able to broach the subject that had brought her to the big-house. And when Miss Adelaide heard her request for work, she looked amazed.

'I'd like to have you here with me, Famie,' she said, 'because I know what beautiful ironing you can do, and I've seen your sewing and mending, but you know how it is with us. We employ all niggers. I can't bother with mulattoes, it's too much trouble.'

Famie nodded. She knew what the white woman meant. Mulattoes and negroes do not eat together, although they work together. Miss Adelaide meant that she would not bother with three sets of meals — one for the whites, one for the mulattoes, and a third for the blacks. But Famie persisted, she must have work, and in the end it was settled. Famie came as ironing woman, housemaid, general utility worker at Yucca: she received the usual woman worker's wages, ten dollars a month and her meals. Within a few weeks she was a part of Yucca Plantation, like Mug and Henry-Jack, like the dogs and cats and the pigs and the mules, like the sun and the rain.

Famie came each day to the big-house just as the sun was rising and the dew lay white on grass and clover; she kindled a fire in the kitchen stove, dripped coffee, then carried the tinkling trays to the white folks up-stairs. Each one had a tray to himself, each had a small coffee-pot and a cup, a glass of cool water, a small sugar bowl, a white napkin. First she would go to Mr. Guy's room which smelled of gun-grease and leather, and where he slept in the large four-post bed that had be-longed to his grandfather; it was a large, bare chamber and the door creaked as Famie pushed it open. Next she went into Miss Adelaide's room, all white and yellow, with soft white curtains billowing at the win-dows, and with silver brushes lying on the bureau. Then she went on to the grandmother's room, where the old lady lay like a waxen figure in the large, dark bed, a table filled with books beside her, and with a red-ribbon marker in the Bible. 'Mornin', Famie!' she would say crisply, reaching a blue-veined hand out from under the mosquito netting.

Only these three lived at Yucca during most of the year, but in summer the boys came home from school, and there were many white linen suits to iron.

Barefoot, Famie would stand in the dust under a fig tree near the kitchen door, her thin shoulders bent over the ironing-board, using all of her strength to press the creases into the heavy linen. Above her the thick leaves of the tree shut off the sun, but the heat seemed to come from everywhere — from the charcoal furnace where the irons heated, from the ground, from the very air itself.

At three o'clock in the afternoon quiet descended on the plantation; dinner was over and done with, and the men and mules had gone back to the fields again; Mug had gone home to her cabin down the road, to rest until time to prepare supper; Henry-Jack hoed in the flower-garden, and Famie continued with the ironing. Upstairs the white ladies slept behind bowed green window shutters.

This was the hard part of the day for Famie. She did her work by will power, long after her real strength was exhausted. By evening she was so tired that she would have to sit and rest for a long time before she could walk home.

As she walked homeward in the twilight, she would watch the smoke rising straight into the air from the chimneys of the cabins, and she would smell suppers cooking. Hunger stirred, but she was always too tired to make a fire on the hearth at home; instead, she ate scraps of cold food that she carried home from the kitchen at Yucca. Then, too, her teeth troubled her when she ate hot food. Pain kept one awake and that was bad, for all one's strength is needed for the work of tomorrow. She felt that the night was her friend, and the old hot sun was her enemy.

Her house was a haven of refuge, for it was quiet

there and she could rest. The rooms were empty, the furniture gone. Only one bed remained, and a home-made table and chairs; the washstand of the old bed-room set remained, too. White people didn't use wash-stands any more, Miss Flossie had said, so Famie could keep it. She kept her clothes in a battered trunk, or hanging on the wall. They were all old now, and it didn't matter.

Little by little old ties were broken, and relatives came to call less often. Famie did not think about them any longer. She even forgot to go to the christening of John Javilée's thirteenth grandchild. She was getting more peculiar every day, her cousins said. When John Javilée's oldest grandchild was married, Famie was not invited to the ceremony, and, although she told herself that she would have been too tired to go, she felt the slight.

She began to brood, sitting on the steps of her cabin in the moonlight, or inside beside the empty hearth when the rain pattered down. She would sit for hours without stirring, her hands lying quiet in her lap; some-times she would sigh heavily, hardly knowing why.

But late in the evening, when she heard the mothers calling their children home, she always went through the same ceremony. She would close the batten doors and window blinds, and from the washstand she would take the old blue striped bowl. Her fingers caressing the cool smoothness of the crockery, she would dream: Joel's white body, his soft hair, the feel of his thin knees in her hands. She would sit dreaming until the candle burned itself out. Sometimes she fell asleep in her chair, the bowl in her lap, only to wake hours later, stiff with pain. Then she would undress and creep into bed.

One day, cleaning the floor behind the washstand, she found Joel's bamboo cane with which he had blown bubbles such as white children blow. She was happy all that day.

That night, alone in the cottage, she filled the bowl with water and blew large, shining bubbles, laughing to think how Joel would enjoy them if he were with her — forgetting that Joel had not blown bubbles for years before he went away.

After that the bubbles became a part of the nightly ceremonial.

Time passed: cotton-planting, Easter in the Isle Brevelle Church, a wedding among her cousins, a funeral, flowers blooming in her little garden among tangled weeds, jasmine white and fragrant, such as Joel used to wear behind his ear. Summer, and the dances for the mulattoes, and shouting and singing in the negro church. Life passed slowly on Cane River, days seemed to linger. August came with the negro baptizings, and the cotton grew tall in the fields again. August with the long, hot, dusty days, when even the leaves of the trees hung straight down, limp in the simmering heat, and when chickens dragged their wings on the ground. The smell of decaying summer hung over everything, sickly sweet, sour, the odor of rotting fruit, and even the sluggish river seemed to give off an unhealthy odor. Then the first cotton boll, white fields, moonlight, cotton-picking, men and women in the furrows, cries for the flatboat, the sound of the cotton-wagons rumbling toward the gin. Money again for the negroes after all these long months. Then the first frost, the first fire, quiet months and easier work, Christmas...

Letters came but seldom from Joel, although every month Famie sent her wages to him. It was cold in Chicago, he wrote, and the work was hard. He worked part of each day as a dishwasher in a restaurant, and his hands were blistered from having them in hot water all the time; he hoped for an easier job soon. He was using the money she sent him to go to night school. Someday he was coming home again.

She read these letters over and over in her cottage at night, and yet they always seemed news from a stranger. Joel was still a small white boy, to be bathed and mothered, kissed and comforted.

Her hands had become knotted and rough, her finger-nails broken. Lines appeared between her eyes. Toothache made the nights hideous with pain, despite the fact that two of her teeth were gone now, pulled by the traveling dentist who came twice a year to the commissary.

Because she did her work well and uncomplainingly, Famie was imposed upon. Twenty times each day she was interrupted to perform some trifling task which belonged by rights to Mug or to Henry-Jack. She did these tasks without thinking about them.

When there was company at the big-house, there were more clothes to iron. Sometimes she admired the delicate silks and sheer organdies of the women's dresses, caressing them with her roughened fingers. Guests sometimes talked with her, asking questions, but they found such conversation an uphill journey. Mug, black and jovial, would sing and pat and even dance a few lumbering steps for company. Everyone liked her, found her amusing, tipped her liberally. But Famie never sulked, nor even appeared to notice; she accepted what was offered without question, and sent it, along with her wages, to Joel.

Day by day she grew more like the negroes among whom she worked: exposure darkened her skin, and nowadays she tied her head up in a *tignon* as negro women do, to avoid the trouble of combing their hair each day. Nowadays, too, she ate with the negroes in the kitchen.

At first she had been diffident, taking her plate of food outside, and eating alone under the fig trees, feeding the chickens with the scraps. Later she became more friendly with Mug and Henry-Jack and the other servants who ate in the kitchen, and when her plate was handed to her, she would take it across the room and eat from the window sill; one day she remained at the table with them and ate there. After that it was an accepted custom and her place was laid along with theirs. Old John Javilée, coming to borrow quinine from Miss Adelaide's medicine chest, saw Famie eating with the negroes, and told the news to the other mulattoes. Famie had lost caste, and she no longer cared what people said about her.

She never complained of the food, as the others did sometimes, nor did she say that the white folks took all of the good things and left the bad things for the negroes. When there was unexpected company in the dining-room — which happened oftener and oftener these days — and the food was skimpier than usual in the kitchen, Famie would join the other servants in their low moan that was their joking reproof to the mistress of the house. They would sing:

> White folks in the parlor, eatin' cake an' cream,
> Niggers in de kitchen, eatin' po'k an' greens.

Then came the long moaning refrain:

> Cawnbraid...

White folks ate cornbread too, of course, but the refrain was understood by all who heard it as criticism and appeal.

'What are the niggers singing in the kitchen?' guests would ask, and Miss Adelaide would say: 'Oh, just a song of their own. Nothing much.'

She and Mr. Guy would exchange glances, then Miss Adelaide would rise and unlock the preserve-closet. She would take a jar of preserved figs into the kitchen, where, without a word, she would put it on the table. Mug and Jack would guffaw, and Famie would smile and roll her eyes.

As time went on, Famie became more and more absent-minded; she worked mechanically, steadily, but she was always 'wool-gathering' as Miss Adelaide called it.

'Good Lord, Famie, this is the second time today that I've found you sweeping the gallery. You're day-dreaming again. Stop now, and go and do something else. There's enough work to do, goodness knows, without doing any of it twice.'

Famie paused, realized the meaning of the words and said, 'Law, Miss Adelaide, Ah forgets.'

She was always like that, thinking vague thoughts, dreams without substance or direction, all centering around Joel — not Joel the man, but the small white boy that she bathed in her cabin each night.

Once every month she sent money to him in Chicago, and to her wages she added her small tips, her Christmas presents, the dimes she earned doing errands. She seemed tireless. At night she took mending home to her cottage and sewed beside the oil lamp — her 'mulatto lamp,' which in Cane River talk means a clean one, as opposed to a 'nigger lamp,' which designates a dirty one, usually lacking a chimney and flaring dangerously in a tight-shut cabin.

The months passed by, one after another, nearly all alike. Joel's letters were formal and stilted, and so were her replies. He always asked for money, and she always sent all that she had. His news was scanty. He had finished night school and had taken another job; it was better work, but the pay was poor. Prospects, however, were good, and he hoped someday to go to New York where a friend had gone and was prospering ... 'Well, I will come to a close. This will be all from your son Joel Vidal. P.S. Don't forget to send me a little extra money if you can spare it. Times are hard here.'

# CHAPTER XXIII

FAMIE never regained the standing that she had lost among her own kind. Her cousins passed her by and wished her the time of day, but she was avoided now. Her cottage, in the curve of the river, was set far back from the road and few passed close to it. Night after night she sat alone on the bench under the China tree in the moonlight, listening to the shouts of the negroes in the fields. Surrounded by life, she was apart from it, a listener only. She felt that she was no longer a mulatto, nor was she a negro; she was nothing.

Her hands coarsened, her back bent. She was not yet thirty-five years old, but she was beginning to look like an old woman. Once, white visitors at Yucca called her 'Auntie.'

On his fifth Christmas away from Cane River, Joel sent his mother his photograph. It was waiting in the commissary post-office when she went to mail her monthly letter to him. She clutched the package in her hand and hurried away. As soon as she was out of sight of the store, she began to run, and alone in her cottage, panting, breathless, she opened it. Tears blurred her eyes so that she could not see it at first. At last she gave a smothered cry: 'Jesus...'

For Joel was a strange white man, dressed in white folks' style, like the pictures of Mr. Guy's friends in the parlor at Yucca. No, that could never be Joel. She hid the picture away, showed it to nobody. Sometimes she took it out in the evening and studied it, but she always put it away again and resumed her dreaming.

Every night she would bar the door and place the lamp upon the mantel. Then she kindled a small fire on the hearth and put the copper kettle upon it. The blue-ringed washbowl was placed upon the floor, where it left a wet ring on the white-scrubbed boards. Warm water was poured in, then cool water was added. Famie sat upon the floor, pressing her hands upon the edge of the bowl. She breathed quickly, and closed her eyes — it seemed that Joel stood before her, young, naked, shivering — slowly her hands moved over the curved surface of the china, slipping slowly into the tepid water... Joel was there... In a moment she would have his white body in her arms.

Nothing in her daily life was as real as this dream. She lived all day for this moment, waiting. The

ecstasy began when her fingers first closed upon the
curved coolness of the bowl's edge. She imagined that
she could feel the blue rim; it was of a different texture
from the smooth white of the bowl itself . . . His body
was white and soft . . . She felt guilty and ashamed and
happy.

Sometimes she could not evoke this ecstasy; then she
would fall face down upon the floor, crying aloud, beating her head against the boards.

One day, while she was ironing under the fig tree, she
felt a sharp pain in her side. She fell down in the dust,
moaning. Nobody heard, for it was mid-afternoon and
the whole plantation seemed asleep. After a time she
was able to drag herself to her feet again and go on with
her work.

The pains came frequently after that, and she grew
to know the meaning of agony, and to wait for the pain,
wincing. She lived like a woman drugged, hardly thinking at all, working like a machine.

She grew more inarticulate, and daily she grew more
like the negroes around her. She became superstitious,
trying their charms and spells, wearing a nutmeg on a
string around her neck to cure pains in her head, and a
cord, knotted nine times, was tied around her waist to
ease the pain in her side.

Mug, the cook, noticing that Famie pressed her hand
to her heart, suggested a remedy: 'Yo' got tuh catch

yo'seff three frogs in a cemetery and den put 'em alive in a red-hot i'on pot. Den, when dey dead, yo' lettum cool off and rub yo'seff wid de frog-grease. Dat'll sho' fix yo'.'

Famie tried it, as she tried many similar remedies. Like the negroes she had become slovenly at home: she no longer reddened the hearth with pounded brick-dust, she no longer scrubbed the floor-boards white and clean. Cobwebs hung in the corners and there was a gaping hole in the mosquito-*baire*, where mosquitoes whined in and out. Nobody but Henry Tyler came to the cottage any more, and he didn't count.

Her feet hurt, and she took to cutting her shoes as negroes do. Nowadays she shuffled as she walked. At night she sat alone for hours, unmoving, staring into the dark before her, her hands lying in her lap.

Joel had been away six years.

Miss Adelaide was telling Flossie about Famie: 'I believe that she's getting deaf, probably from all that trouble with her teeth. And then, of course, she never pays any attention, just lives in a trance. She's got so now that she doesn't say, "What's that?" or "Ma'am?" as the others do when they don't hear what I say. Instead she says, "Do what?" Always just that. Yes, indeed, Flossie, they all have their little peculiarities.'

Miss Adelaide was fond of generalities about negroes, but Flossie was in no mood for such discussion.

'Speaking of peculiarities,' she said, 'I wonder if she has any funny old things in the attic of her house? I never thought to ask her when we bought her other things. You know, Adelaide, there's no telling what she's got *hidden away* up there. Let's go home with her this afternoon and climb up there and look. There's no telling *what* we might find.'

'Shucks,' said Miss Adelaide, 'she's got nothing worth having up there. Only some old, broken things probably. As I was saying, Flossie, she has her own little peculiarities, but she's the best servant I've ever had. Of course she's always wool-gathering, and she doesn't listen, but she's so good and faithful that I don't mind. She never misses a day, rain or shine. And she wouldn't be Famie if she weren't dreaming about something or other.'

Washing at Yucca had grown so heavy that summer that Aunt Dicey assisted three days each week at the tubs under the fig trees — the same clothes that were ironed afterward by Famie. Aunt Dicey was gossiping with Mug as she stirred the steaming wash-pot with a wooden pole.

'Whatcha reckon Miss Famie do, all by husseff in her house at night?'

Mug's eyes widened and her smile disappeared before the tone of the older woman. She glanced over her shoulder before she answered: 'What she do?'

'Well, Ah was a-comin' home from chu'ch Sunday night . . .' she began mysteriously, 'an' Ah heerd a sort-a laughin' inside her house. 'Nough to scare yo' . . . all so still, and de house shut up tight. Ah sort-a listened, and den Ah open de gate easy, an' Ah goes in. A streak o' light was comin' out of a crack by de chimley, an' Ah peep in . . . an' she was a-sittin' on de flo' wid a little cane in her hands. She was sort-a playin' wid a wash-bowl, an' . . . she was blowin' bubbles!'

'Fo' Gawd!' cried Mug, her eyes distended, her mouth open. 'What else yo' see, Aunt Dicey?'

'An' den she got to laughin' an' clappin' her hands, an' *talkin' to somethin' that wa'n't theah!*'

'Oh, Jesus!'

'Ah heerd her say: "Look, baby," an' then, "Look, white boy." An' she laugh agin . . . an' dey wasn't a soul aroun'.' The old woman's voice fell into a husky whisper: '*Dat's conjure doin's.*'

But Mug shook her head scornfully and sadly.

'Um-ump,' she said in negation, 'Famie ain't no witch, Aunt Dicey, she's jus' dreamin' about Joel. She's gettin' ole an' she forgits he's gone, an' ain't nevah comin' back.'

'Ole? Ole!' Dicey shook her head and the gold hoops in her ears flopped to and fro: 'Famie ain't ole. She's as young as yo' is, an' she's heaps younger than my gal Bessie. What yo' talkin' bout, Mug?'

''Tain't only clocks an' calendars that make yo' ole.'

Dicey grunted and turned without a word to her washtub, while Mug went singing through the sunlight toward the vegetable-garden where the watermelons were turning green, and where tomatoes hung heavy, shining red against rich brown earth. Her voice, uplifted to her Jesus, came back in reproof to the old gossip:

> Let's have a time, oh, let's have a time,
> Chatterin' wid de angels...
> Let's have a time!

In the kitchen, where she was cleaning silver beside the open window, Famie smiled. Often now she caught herself with a negro baptizing hymn on her lips. The songs comforted her someway, with their mournful cadences.

Upstairs, Miss Adelaide was darning stockings as she talked with Flossie: 'Listen!' she said.

'Chattering with the angels, *what* an idea!' said Flossie; 'you know, Adelaide, I believe that I'll begin collecting these negro spirituals. They're so *quaint.*'

Mug, returning from the garden, her blue apron full of red and shining tomatoes, and her black face glistening with sweat, passed Dicey and added further admonition by singing another verse of the hymn:

> Mary had a virgin Son,
> The cruel Jews done had him hung...
> He had a time... Oh, He had a time...
> Chatterin' wid de angels, He had a time.

Dicey, reproved for her gossip, pounded the clothes in the tub with such gusto that buttons were scraped off against the washboard. She grunted aloud: 'Humph!'

'Why, of co'se, Henry, Ah'm glad to mend it fo' yo'. Heah, it's finish'.'

Famie rose from beside the lamp in her cottage and handed the faded blue overalls to the man who lounged in the doorway, relaxed, weary from his long day behind mule and plow.

'Ah hates to ask yo', ti'ed as Ah know yo' is,' he said.

Famie made a gesture: 'Law, Henry, but Ah'm glad. Yo' been doin' things fo' me all yeah, an' this is the firs' time Ah've had a chance to do anything fo' yo'.'

It was true that Henry Tyler had been Famie's friend for a long time now. She had come to depend upon his strength. He cut wood for her in winter, and helped her with the heavier tasks. Tonight he had come to ask her to patch a torn garment, and she had been working for half an hour while he sat watching her.

Since his wife died, and his sons had gone away, he was lonely. His house was ill-kept and dirty, and he cooked his own food. He never forgot his talks with Mr. Paul, and night after night, he sat looking at the stars wondering why things must be as they were. Once, he thought he had found the answer, but that time was past. Now he wanted to talk with Famie, to ask her questions, but he was ashamed, remembering the difference between them, knowing that, in her eyes, he was of another race. He knew that her friends looked down upon him, knew that he brought criticism upon her by coming to her house, knew that only harm could come to her through their relationship. These were the things that he wanted to tell her, to explain to her. She was always friendly, always grateful for the things he did for her, and he wanted her to know that he did not wish to cause trouble, that it was only his desire to help that brought him to her cottage ... These things were hard to say, and he couldn't find the words.

She handed him the mended overalls, and together they went out into the summer night.

Now, as they stood looking at the moonlit river, he felt desire for her, he wanted to take her in his arms, to hold her, to make her his woman. The sudden passion frightened him, yet he knew that he had felt the need of her for a long time now.

The warm night was vibrant with the song of many insects, and from the river came the chorus of croaking frogs. An odor sickly sweet hung in the air.

Famie drew in her breath and said: 'Ah can smell the caterpillars in the cotton ...'

'We goin' start poisonin' 'em tonight,' Henry said. 'Mister Guy's sent fo' me to come at ten o'clock.'

She thought of the invisible horde of insects in the young green leaves of the cotton plants, advancing across the acres, destroying the crop. The odor that filled the air was from the cut and broken leaves of cotton stalks. Unless poison was spread for them, the caterpillars would continue their advance until the whole crop was destroyed.

Boll-weevils, storms, caterpillars, all were enemies of cotton, and enemies of men. Life in the fields was a continuous struggle, and someday the enemy would defeat them all. The fields would be bare and brown and no smoke would rise from the chimneys any more. Children would be hungry ... She sighed.

One needed strength to fight these things. It was the old familiar, back-breaking battle that she had known since childhood. One needed courage to keep on.

'We'll be poisonin' f'om now till daylight,' Henry told her as he turned away.

'Where?' she asked, feeling that she would like to do something to make the long night easier for him.

'In the eas' fiel'.' He made a gesture toward the dark.

'Ah've got lots o' mendin' to do,' she said, 'and Ah'll be up late. If yo' wants me to, Ah'll bring yo' some coffee 'bout two o'clock.'

It was after midnight when Famie put aside her sewing and wiped her eyes. A pile of mended garments lay on the floor beside her chair, and she folded them away. Far off in the field she could hear the whining of the poison machine; it was coming nearer as the moments passed. She kindled a fire and put the water on to boil, then took two cups from the shelf. Before long the room was filled with the fragrant aroma of coffee. When she had dripped enough, she took the cups and the pot and went outside.

The westering moon was shining as she went toward the east field. It was not far, and she could tell the position of the workers by the hovering cloud of white that hung, settling, over the cotton. The whining was coming nearer, and she walked down to the turn-row and waited. The cotton was waist-high and dew glittered on it. The machine had done its work well, and she could see the fine film of powdered arsenic caught and held upon the wet leaves ... When the caterpillars reached this part of the field, they would die by thousands.

Presently she saw the slow-moving wagon in the distance coming toward her. Two mules dragged it, their heads shrouded in white cotton nosebags. As the wagon-wheels turned, cog-wheels turned the machine, which screamed like a live thing, and a horizontal cloud of finely powdered dust shot out, quivered, and hung in the air, slowly settling. Riding high on the wagon she could see two black men, their faces covered by white muslin masks. How ghostly they seemed, riding there, working the levers which controlled the deadly cloud.

Henry saw her standing at the turn-row and pulled a lever down. The screaming ceased and the wheels were still. It was quiet now as the machine approached her, for the hooves of the mules made no sound on the soft earth.

Famie felt the arsenic in her mouth, in her lungs, and her eyes smarted.

'Go back!' Henry Tyler called. Famie moved farther away, standing so that the lightly moving air would blow the dust away from her.

A slim negro boy jumped down, wiping the white film from his face: 'Law! Miss Famie done brung some coffee.' He was highly pleased.

Famie watched them drink, and watched the tired mules gulp water from buckets which stood by the fence. Henry's black face was covered with a film of white, but he smiled at her as she handed him the steaming cup.

'Ain't nobody else in the world would do dis fo' me,' he said.

'Ah didn' know dat yo' an' Mr. Henry was courtin',' the boy said, smiling.

'Shut yo' mouth,' said Henry Tyler. 'Yo' know betta dan dat. Miss Famie's a kind-hearted lady ... Yo're a nigger, an' Ah'm a nigger. She feel sorry fo' us.'

Famie was startled: she had not thought that such an interpretation might be put upon her simple act of kindness. She brushed the unpleasant idea of gossip from her mind. What difference did it make?

'Drink yo' coffee, boy,' she said, 'Ah've got to go.'

# CHAPTER XXIV

OUTSIDE the kitchen door at Yucca, in the shade of a tree, Famie sat mending rough-dried clothes; after dinner she would begin to iron them, but now she waited for Mug to call her into the kitchen to help serve the midday meal to Mr. Guy and Miss Adelaide.

All morning the guinea-hens had been crying like the rusty hinges of a swinging door, but now they were quiet. In the vegetable-garden near-by Henry-Jack was setting out tomato plants. The sunlight was warm and he had taken off his shirt and spread it on a little bush to dry; his black body, naked to the waist, glistened with sweat as he crouched upon the brown earth.

Famie was listening to the chorus that lifted its voice to welcome summer; the ever-changing song of mocking-birds, the sharp cawing of the jays as they fought and made love in the tree above her head; in the dovecote the pigeons cooed without ceasing, always the same few notes, broken by the clattering of their claws on the roof, as some of them returned from expeditions to the orchard. The hens, too, were clucking — each hen followed by a brood of downy yellow chicks — and a rooster flapped his wings and crowed. Far off she could hear the sharp metallic note of the grackle, and from its hidden perch in some near-by tree came the plaint of the mourning dove: *Ou-hoo-hoo-hoo-hoo*, like a young girl crying.

Then, as she listened, she heard an undercurrent of sound: thousands of insects, crickets, katydids, the buzzing of wasps, the droning of bees; and then, the shrilling of locusts rising like the wind of an approaching storm, then dying away in a falling cadence, fainter, fainter, until lost in the medley of sound which supplanted it.

Mr. Guy's black-and-white female setter — the one which was gun-shy and, consequently, in eternal disgrace — lay sleeping at Famie's feet, lulled by the familiar sounds of early summer.

Suddenly, from beyond the river, came a heavy detonation, ominous, and dulled by the distance.

Boom!

The chorus of birds and insects was silent; every living thing was still, waiting.

Again the detonation came, louder, like a crash of thunder.

The dog came whimpering to Famie and cowered against her skirt, and she put her hand upon the animal's head. They waited together, the dog in fear, the woman in wonder. What could it be, this sound of war in a quiet, peaceful land?

But there was only silence, and the bird notes began again: first a few chirruping calls, then a long, low trill, and another and another bird joined until the air was full of song; insect voices called, the locusts began their cry, and the chickens and pigeons went about their business of life as before.

Only the dog was still worried, and she licked Famie's hand and looked up at her face. 'It's all right,' the woman said. 'Nothin' ain't goin' to hu't yo'.'

Henry-Jack came swaggering by, a large basket balanced on his head. Famie called to him, asking what the explosion was.

'It's de road-builders,' he said. 'Blastin' out stumps on the river bank,' and then, calling back over his shoulder, 'Ah specks they'll be heah befo' many days.'

Mr. and Mrs. Randolph were in the dining-room; it was dim and cool there, but through the open windows they could see bushes of bridal-wreath white in the sunlight.

'Where's the clerk?' Miss Adelaide asked. 'His soup is getting cold.'

'He's sorting out the mail,' her husband said. 'I told

him to do it before he came over, so that the mail-rider won't be held up longer than necessary; he's late, anyway, because the road is torn up on the other side of the river.'

Miss Adelaide nodded. 'You know,' she said, 'I'm almost sorry to see the new road come to Yucca and Isle Brevelle. Things will never be the same with a highway before our door. Years ago I used to long for such a road, but now I'm afraid of it, someway. Everything will change.'

'It will double the value of the plantation,' said Mr. Guy. 'All these river acres will be worth more in a year or two. But I see what you mean ... the negroes will get demoralized. I've seen it happen in other places. In that sense, I'm sorry, too. But it will be fine to be able to drive to town in less than an hour, instead of taking half a day and breaking an automobile spring every trip.'

Miss Adelaide laughed. 'I remember the first automobile that ever came here,' she said; 'it was Flossie and Harry Smith. You remember, don't you, Guy? Mug got so excited that she let the gumbo boil over.'

'Yes, I remember; but do you know, Addie, that's been twenty years ago. Little Guy was a baby, and John wasn't born.'

The clerk came in and put a bundle of mail down by Miss Adelaide's plate, then took his place at the table.

'Thanks,' she said, as she began to sort out the letters:

'Seed catalogues, circulars ... Here's a letter from Flossie — speaking of angels ——' She tore the flap of the envelope open, read a few lines hastily, then said: 'She and Harry are coming for Easter. Good Lord, Guy, they've got another new car, a Packard this time, she says. They have a new one every time they come, it seems to me.'

She was about to put the letters aside, but stopped to say: 'Why, that's strange. Why did you bring this letter to me?'

'Which one is that?' the clerk asked. 'Oh, I wanted to give it to Famie. It looks as though it might be important.'

'Famie?' said Mr. Guy. 'Let's see.'

Miss Adelaide passed the letter across to him, and he said: 'That's funny.'

'What's funny?'

'It's from some law firm in Chicago,' her husband said. 'Sloan, Wolfe and Levy, ever hear of them?'

'No, I'm sure I never did,' said his wife. 'You know, Guy, I'll bet that no-account white-nigger Joel of hers is in some sort of trouble. He must be at least twenty years old now, and do you know, she still sends him money.'

'We still send Guy money,' said her husband, smiling.

'Well, if you're trying to tell me that it's none of my business, I'll grant you're right,' Miss Adelaide said, 'but it makes me so mad, just the same ...'

'Sh-sh!' said Mr. Guy, as Famie came into the room with a plate of hot biscuits.

'Don't you *shush* me,' said Miss Adelaide in mock-anger to her husband. 'We were talking about you, Famie, because you have a letter here. Take it, it looks as though it might be important.'

'Fo' me?'

'Yes, here it is. It's from some lawyers in Chicago.'

Two days later Mr. Guy and Famie sat facing each other in the office of the commissary. A fly was buzzing against the window-pane as he read the well-thumbed letter from the Chicago attorneys.

'Of course you realize that he has no right to his share in the property until after your death,' Mr. Guy said. 'That property is yours, every acre of it. You inherited it from old Bizette, and it was originally part of *Grandpère* Augustin's plantation. He can't make you sell it unless you want to.'

'Yessuh, Ah know,' she said, 'but Ah always tole him he could have it when he was a man.'

'What do your relatives say?'

'Ole John Javilée want to buy it,' said Famie, 'an' Madame Aubert Rocque say Ah ought to let him have it, ef Ah'm sellin' it. But they ain't got no cash-money, Mister Guy.'

'Did Javilée tell you what he thought the land was worth?'

'Yessuh, he say it worth mo' than two thousan' dolla's, but...'

'Well, it's not worth more than seven hundred and fifty dollars to me,' said Mr. Guy, 'but that's cash. If you want to sell and if you want the cash at once, I can get it for you. It will be a cash sale, and I don't want you saying that I cheated you. I've already looked into the title, and it's clear.'

Famie nodded. 'Mister Guy, will yo' write to them white men...' she indicated the letter.

'You mean that you'll accept seven hundred and fifty dollars?'

'Yessuh, ef Joel's willin'. It's fo' him.'

'You mean that you are going to give him half?'

'No, suh, it's fo' him.'

'You mean all of it?'

'Yessuh, yo' can tell him it's fo' him.'

Mr. Guy started to speak, but thought better of it; instead he said something different.

'Listen, Famie, I'm not going to get into any lawsuits with your Joel. He's been in Chicago for nearly seven years now, and he got a legal firm to write this letter asking for his share in your property. Now, if you want to sell it, all right, but Joel will have to come here and sign a release. I don't trust lawyers.'

'Joel come heah?'

'Yes, I'll stipulate that in my letter to these... er ... gentlemen in Chicago.'

'Joel come back heah?'

'Yes, that's what I mean. Wouldn't you like to see him after all this time?'

'Oh, yessuh, Mister Guy.'

'I'll write the letter today, then. But let me repeat it again, so I'm sure I've got it straight. You're willing to sell your place, all of it, to me for seven hundred and fifty dollars. And you intend turning this money over to Joel.'

'Yessuh.'

'Why don't you keep some of it, Famie? You're getting older, and you may need it.'

'No, suh, Ah promise...'

'Well, how about that property that Numa left? You're entitled to something there when old Madame Lacour dies.'

'No, suh, Ah done signed a paper.'

'When did you do such a foolish thing as that?'

'Right after Numa die, they come to me...'

'Then there's all the more reason for your keeping some of this money for your old age. Keep it, don't give it all to Joel.'

'No, suh, Ah'll give it...'

Mr. Guy thought for a moment, then said: 'Oh, maybe you're going off with him. Maybe you'll go and live in the North, too.'

'Suh?'

'I said that maybe you'd go and live with Joel in Chicago.'

She was still for a moment, watching the fly buzzing against the pane.

'Ah don' know, suh, but that's what he promise me, long time ago.'

'Do you want me to say that in this letter that I'm going to write?'

'No, suh.'

'Sure he'll remember, are you?'

'Yessuh, Ah'm pretty sho' he will.'

On Sunday afternoon Famie received a message that old Madame Aubert Rocque wanted to see her. When she arrived at the house she found two horses tied to the garden fence, and John Javilée's dilapidated surrey hitched under the big pecan tree; she knew, by these signs, that a group was gathered inside. As she paused by the gate she felt that eyes were watching her from behind the faded blue-green shutters.

She was thin and bent, in her shabby black dress and sunbonnet, and looked like some frail old woman as she stood hesitating beside tall shrubs of shimmering white bridal-wreath and crimson flowering quince. The house was tight shut, keeping its secrets, but she felt the eyes upon her as she went up the path to the door and rapped with a shaking hand upon the faded panels.

Inside it was so dark that Famie could scarcely see. Madame Aubert sat in an armchair, with other old women gathered around her. In the shadows Famie could see three old men standing. There was a murmur as she entered, but nobody spoke to her.

She went to kiss her great-aunt, but the old woman waved her away. Tersely she told Famie why she had been summoned: her relatives wished to speak to her for the last time.

Standing with her back against the door, Famie heard old John Javilée's voice speaking in a tone that she had never heard him use before.

'Yo' wouldn't let yo' own kin people buy yo' land. No, yo' got to have cash money, an' yo' want it now. We could get together and buy it, maybe if yo' give us time. But yo' can't wait. So yo' goin' to sell it to Mister Guy.'

She tried to answer, but he went on speaking: 'Land is all we got left. It's all we got to keep us from bein' like the niggers. It's our land, an' it's all a part of what *Grandpère* Augustin lef' to us. Little by little white folks is gettin' it all. They're pushin' us out. An' you're helpin' 'em. Yo' sell yo' part of *Grandpère* Augustin's land fo' nothin'. Everybody know it wuth double what yo' gettin' fo' it. An' why yo' sell it? Why?'

'Ah always promise Joel . . .'

'Joel! Yas, yo' son. Yo' think Joel's goin' to take yo' Nawth. Well, wait an' see. He's comin', an' he'll take his money an' go. An' where'll yo' be? Yo' ain't got no kin-people heah no mo' . . . Yo' friends is all niggers . . .'

Famie appealed to her great-aunt: '*Nainaine* . . .'

But the old woman interrupted her. She spoke

rapidly in French and the words stung like the flicks of a lash. Famie, she said, had gone down a hill that she could not climb up again. She had been bad in her youth and she had been forgiven for it. Her relatives had rallied around her and had saved her good name. Numa had married her, but she had neglected him for her white bastard child. Her kin-people had forgiven her for that, too, but they did not forget. Since her boy had gone away, she had outraged them all by her association with negroes. John Javilée had seen her eating with them in the kitchen at Yucca. At church people sneered at her behind her back, and pretended not to see her, but Famie was a fool and didn't even notice. Now people said that black Henry Tyler was her lover. Madame Aubert Rocque refused to believe it until proof was brought to her. People had seen him leave her house late at night, and she sewed for him, and even brought coffee to him in the field, like any negro woman waiting on her man. It was too much. This was the end. They had called her today to tell her so. If she sold her land to Mister Guy, it was better that she go away, go with Joel or alone, it didn't matter. They had sent Nita away because she had disgraced them, and now Famie had humbled them all. Her name had become a byword, and men laughed at her when they talked together. She was a traitor to her people, and she made her relatives ashamed that her name was the same as theirs.

Dully, Famie listened, looking from one to another. Numa's mother was crying, her face buried in her hands, but Madame Aubert Rocque sat up stiff and stern. She was very old, very withered, but she had the dignity of a matriarch. The weight of ninety-five years had not broken her spirit.

Famie felt herself trembling. She leaned back against the door and tried to find words with which to answer. This was her own aunt, this was her grandmother's own sister who was speaking to her so bitterly. But today the old woman was the representative of a proud race that had been outraged; family ties were forgotten in the disgrace which she felt Famie had brought upon them.

The old woman rose, her fichu falling to the floor, and, ashen and shaking, she pointed with her cane to the portrait of *Grandpère* Augustin which hung on the wall.

'His own great-great-granddaughter disgracin' him. Yo'! My own sister Odalie's gran'chile! Ah'm through with yo'. If yo' meet me in the road, don't speak to me.'

Staggering, she fell back in her chair, and the other old women gathered around her; Numa's mother held a glass of water to her lips. The old men came forward out of the shadows.

Famie heard a confused murmur of voices. Someone took her by the elbow and pushed her outside the door. She heard the door close behind her. She was alone in the sunlit garden. She stood with her hand against her lips, looking about her, seeing nothing. Useless to protest, useless to say anything, it was all finished, done with. She was insulted, shut out, and they had not let her answer.

But, after all, what could she say? How could she explain the purpose to which she had given everything? How could she tell them that her own degradation had come because Joel had risen? Nothing could make them understand that the purpose had become interlaced in the very fabric of her life, a part of every move she made, of every breath she drew. Too late to try to tell them now, there were no words that could explain. They were forcing her out of their group, out of their protection; they were pushing her down into the world of negroes. But Joel had escaped. Her purpose was accomplished. They told her she had failed. No!

She swayed as she went down the path to the gate. The sunlight hurt her eyes. Her sunbonnet was gone; she must have dropped it on the floor in the house. It didn't matter.

As she paused to open the gate, she looked back at the house and again she felt the eyes upon her. She knew that the old people were gathered there, peering through the chinks of the shutters, whispering together, looking at her for the last time.

Suddenly she was proud. She shook the tears from her eyes. Let them look at her now.

She broke a sprig of red quince flowers from the bush

beside the gate. Slowly she put it in her hair, adjusted it, squared her shoulders. With steady step, and with her head held high, she walked through the gate and down the road.

# CHAPTER XXV

GUY RANDOLPH looked up from his account-book and saw a stranger standing in the office door, a tall, red-haired young man who wore a well-cut gray suit.

'You wanted to see me?'

'Don't you recognize me, Mister Guy? I'm Joel Vidal.'

'No!' said Mr. Guy.

Joel came into the office and sat in the chair that the planter indicated. 'I caught a ride over from Cypress,' he said. 'I came as soon as I got your letter.'

'Your mother will be glad to see you, Joel.'

'Yes, it's been seven years since I've seen Cane River.'

There was a pause while Mr. Guy looked at the younger man. 'I'll be damned,' he said to himself, 'he's as white as I am. Good-looking, too, but shifty-eyed.

And his clothes are better than my sons wear. He's
quit saying "sir" when he speaks to me.'

'Have you seen your mother yet?' he asked.

'No, I came straight to you. The man who drives the
mail truck let me off here at the store.'

'You're here to see about your mother's property. I
told you in my letter the price I'd pay. Seven hundred
and fifty dollars, cash in hand.'

'Today?'

'Aren't you in a hurry?'

'I'd like to get to my job as soon as I can.'

'What sort of work do you do?'

Joel's eyes shifted: 'Clerical work . . . and some sales
work, too.'

'He's lying,' Mr. Guy thought. 'Well, it's none of my
business.' Aloud he said: 'I'll telephone for my lawyer
to come out from town, and we'll get your mother here.
You understand that the property is hers, not yours.
Legally, you've got no claim to it, but I want your
signature on the deed of sale.'

'That's what I understood.'

Mr. Guy turned a small handle and the telephone
tinkled. He gave a number, and presently Joel heard
him say: 'Ned? This is Guy Randolph. Can you drive
out here to Yucca and bring the papers on that Vidal
land I'm buying? Yes, right away. All right. Listen.
Stop at the bank and get Armstrong to send me seven
hundred and fifty dollars in cash. Oh, it doesn't matter

... twenties will be all right. I'll telephone to him and I'll send the check back by you. Sure, he'll do it. I'll phone him to have it ready when you get there. I'll expect you by four o'clock.'

He called the bank, then turned back to Joel again.

'Don't you want to see your mother while you're waiting? You'll find her over at the big-house. She was ironing in the back yard at dinner time, and you'll probably find her there. Tell her I said that she can take the rest of the day off. I know she wants to talk to you.'

The sale was over, Famie had received her money, and she and Joel were on their way home. Negroes in the commissary and in the road stared curiously at the sight of the well-dressed white man and the shabby mulatto woman walking together.

'Good-night, Miss Famie.'

'Good-night, Mug.'

'Good-night.'

''Night, Henry-Jack.'

Joel nodded to them, but said nothing. He kept on walking as though he were in a hurry.

She was glad when they turned into the path which led to her gate. The path went between weeds, and canes grew high along the fences; as the years had passed the house had become dark from the growth around it.

She fumbled with the old rag which tied the gate;

she felt as though she were bringing a stranger home with her.

'Ah'm sorry Ah didn't know yo' was comin' today,' she said. 'The house is plum dirty.'

They crossed the threshold, and Joel said: 'Why, it's empty. What did you do with all our furniture?'

She shrugged her shoulders: 'Ah sold it.' She felt that she could not tell him that the proceeds from the sale had kept him for the first few months he had been away. He asked no further question, but walked from room to familiar room.

'It seems smaller than I remembered it, different someway,' he said. He stood in the doorway looking out at the river, the church on the opposite shore, and at the thicket farther along the bank.

'The river looks the same, though,' he said.

They sat down in the doorway, their feet on the rotting steps which led down to the water. She tried to tell him of the happenings in the neighborhood since he had gone away, of births, marriages, deaths among her relatives. He had forgotten most of the people she mentioned.

Long silences fell between them. The cottage shamed him; it was mouldy and shabby and there were dirty quilts on the unmade bed. Only the blue-rimmed wash-bowl was as it had always been.

'I never see a bubble that I don't think of that bowl,' he said. 'It's strange, as I think of it. You wanted me to blow bubbles because Mr. Guy's sons did. Why did you want that?'

She could not answer, nor could she answer the other questions he asked her. His narrowed cold blue eyes embarrassed her. She was glad that the daylight was fading.

In his way he tried to be gentle with her, but disgust was in his nostrils; the odor of poverty and squalor hung over everything. He was glad that he would not have to sleep there. Mr. Guy, friendly at the last, had said that he would have someone take him to the night train, six miles away. He seemed relieved that Joel wanted to go at once. There had been no mention of Famie's future plans, nor had she thought beyond the moment.

When black-dark came Famie lighted the lamp, took the money from her knotted handkerchief, and handed it to Joel.

'It's fo' yo', son,' she said.

Joel counted the money, hesitated, then said: 'But don't you need some of it?'

'What call Ah got fo' money?'

'Well, I can use it all right,' he said, and he put the roll of bills into his pocket.

After a time he said: 'Mr. Guy said you expected to go away with me. That's not true, is it?'

'What's that yo' say, son?'

'You're not planning to leave Cane River, are you?' he asked. 'Mr. Guy said something like that to me, but

I told him that you didn't want to leave. This is home to you. All your friends and kin-people are here.'

Friends? She had no friends, no kin-people, but she could not tell Joel that. And now she knew that he did not want her either. But, as she looked at him, she felt no rancor, no bitterness, for this strange, narrow-eyed white man was not her boy. This man was a stranger. Joel was the small boy that she still bathed in the wash-bowl each night. She continued to look at him, but she made no reply.

'I was sure of that,' he said. 'And it's the only possible thing. You see, it's like this . . . I may as well tell you about it. I've left Chicago for good and all, and I'm going to California where I don't know anybody at all. I've crossed the line in Chicago, but it's dangerous there. Too many people know that I'm not all white. On the coast, nobody will ever know. I'm going, and I'm breaking off clean with the people I've known. This money will do it for me. That's why I wanted it now, not later.'

This, then, was the end. She tried to talk to him, to say something, anything.

'Where yo' goin' to live, son?'

He bit his lip, and she understood. He did not want her to know. It was better, safer that way.

Joel was gone.

The moon shone down softly through the gathering

mist and the cotton-field was a milky sea. Layers of air, now warm, now cool, rose from the river. Famie sat in the doorway, her head bowed upon her knees. She was like a woman drugged, she felt nothing, thought nothing. She only knew that she was very tired and that she could rest.

In the deep shade of the China tree Henry Tyler sat watching her. He had crept close — just as he had crept close to Mr. Paul's cabin long ago — impelled by a doglike emotion that he could not name, but he knew that she needed him.

For hours the woman sat there unmoving, but at last she lifted her head, and from the darkness Henry could see her brushing back a lock of hair from her forehead. Presently she rose unsteadily and went indoors.

Henry crept closer. He saw her looking dully around the room, saw her start toward a corner, hesitate, then move forward again. She was standing in the lamplight with her hands upon the rim of the blue-and-white wash-bowl, her eyes closed. She was preparing for bed, he thought, and was about to turn away when he was arrested by the sound of her voice.

'No.'

He saw her lift the bowl high above her head, and send it crashing down upon the hearth.

# CHAPTER XXVI

A VOICE was calling her name and Famie rose reluctantly from the deep well of sleep. It was dark in the cottage, but moonlight shone blue outside the window. Framed in the bright rectangle of the open door was the silhouette of a man's figure.

'Who... what yo' want?' she asked.

'Dis is Henry Tyler,' the voice answered. 'Ah done come to tek yo' to chu'ch.'

Then she remembered. She had promised Henry that she would go with him to Easter sunrise service. Their appearance would serve as an announcement that their future lives would be spent together, and everyone would know that she had left her own people and had gone to his.

'Sit down, Henry, an' wait while I get dress'.'

Ten minutes later they were riding together on an

old white mule, he in the saddle, she sitting behind on a folded sack, her arm around his waist.

The big-house at Yucca seemed sleeping among its trees, with moonlight slanting across its white columns. Mist hung low over the river, and the foggy fields seemed to end in a white wall of clouds. Slowly the mule went down the river road, and Henry and Famie seemed two ghosts riding. After a mile the mule left the road and went across a cotton-field toward the woods beyond. It was cool, and they could smell the swamp. In the stillness an owl called and Henry shivered and turned his hat backward to ward off bad luck.

The woods loomed ahead, a dark wall. Festoons of Spanish moss were lighter among the shadows, and the moonlight did not penetrate beneath the trees. Henry curbed the mule and turned the animal's head into a trail which led into blackness. Famie could see nothing and rode with her arm raised to protect her face from thorns and branches. From time to time she could feel Henry stoop to avoid a low limb or entangling vine, and she stooped with him, her cheek pressed against his shoulder.

The two-mile ride through the woods seemed endless, but it ended at last. Ahead she could see a clearing with moonlight slanting down on the white rectangular stones of a cemetery. Henry dismounted, and she slid down from the mule's back into his arms. He tied the mule to the graveyard fence. The dark spire of the small church leaned crazily against the lighter sky. It was black under the trees beside the church and she could see nothing, but the darkness was alive with voices.

'Howdy, Mister Henry.'

''Mawnin', Sis Viney.'

'Is de songsters come yet?'

Here and there the burning end of a cigarette or the wider glow of a pipe shone for a moment and faded again. There were many negroes waiting there, and she could feel them around her, although she could not see them. An old woman's voice came from the blackness at her elbow.

''Mawnin', Miss Famie, how yo' do?'

'Who's that? Ah can't see yo'.'

'Lawd Gawd, is Ah so black yo' can't see me?' There came a ripple of deep laughter. 'Dis is Lizzie Balize.'

She felt the old woman's hand upon her arm, and as Lizzie puffed deep on her pipe, for a moment Famie could see her wrinkled face with its scars below her white head-handkerchief.

The crowd was moving toward the church door, and Henry took her elbow and pushed her ahead of him into the blackness of the building. She felt the smooth backs of the benches under her groping fingers, then found an empty pew and slid in, moving over against the wall. The windows were open, and the dying moonlight was pale beyond them. The dark hour before daylight was upon them. Within the church she could hear the scraping of feet on the bare floor, and a dog yelped suddenly as someone stepped on it. There was a murmur of whispering voices.

After a time there came a profound hush and out of the stillness a woman's voice rose in a mournful chant:

Oh, guilty, guilty my mind is,
Oh, take away de stain...

Many women's voices took up the melody and a chorus of men's voices hummed the accompaniment. Only two lines, repeated over and over, then silence again. A woman sobbed aloud, a sob which was quickly muffled. There was a moment of expectancy, then a man's deep voice began to speak:

'Please, Jesus, oh, please, Jesus!'

Twenty voices called out in response from the blackness:

'Hab mussy!'

'Lawd he'p!'

'Oh, Jesus!'

Then the man's voice went on again:

'I want you to tear down de wall. Teach our feets to know the way fo' peace, fo' everlastin' peace.'

Then another man's voice: 'We goin' to ask ole Aunt Dicey to pray fo' us.'

There was a stir, a sound of footsteps, and the old woman's voice was heard: 'O Lawd! It's wid a pure heart Ah comes to Yo' dis mawnin'! Ah pray, an' Ah pray. O Lawd, Yo' done heard me pray, an' now Ah wants Yo' to heah us all pray. We wants Yo' to come among us dis mawnin', Lawd, an' let Yo' light shine upon us. Lawd! Lawd! We is wanderin' 'roun' in de dark, an' we needs Yo' to come an' bring us de sunrise, an' let us see how to walk in de right road. Oh, we needs Yo', Lawd, an' we needs Yo' bad.'

From the congregation there came a chorus of assent:
'Dat's right, Lawd!'
'Jesus, he'p!'
'Hab mussy!'

With a strangled sob the old woman cried: 'Jordan, stand still an' let me cross ovah!'

In the pause that followed, Famie could hear the sound of sobbing, then a woman's voice began a hymn. It was the familiar melody 'Swing Low, Sweet Chariot,' and in the darkness it rang out with almost unbearable beauty. Many were crying now and there were frequent shouts of 'Please, Lawd!' and 'Hab mussy!'

The moonlight had faded out and there was blackness everywhere. Then a new voice was heard, a man's voice, rich and soft. The sermon was beginning:

'The chu'ch is throwed open dis mawnin' an' we done come a long way from home to get heah, but heah we is, Lawd, heah we is!'

Other voices interrupted: 'Yes, Lawd!'
'Heah we is, Lawd!'
'Look at us, Lawd!'

'Lawd, help!'

The preacher spoke again, this time with a strange rhythm:

'Once a yeah we leaves ouh houses while it is still dark, Lawd! Once a yeah we come heah to dis dark chu'ch. We leaves ouh houses an' we comes to Yo'.'

His voice became a sing-song chant:

We comes a long way...
Through de woods an' 'mongst de trees.
We comes slow, slow, but we comes,
'Cause we been thinkin', Lawd,
Yes, thinkin' 'bout Resurrection.
Yes, Lawd, de Resurrection of Jesus!
We thinks 'bout it.
We lies down wid it an' we gits up wid it
'Cause all ouh hopes is built up
On de resurrection of de dead.
Some mens says we dies
An' dies fo' good,
An' some mens says dat we don't git up no mo';
But I don't believe dat, Lawd,
An' my people heah don't believe dat!
No, suh!
If I believed dat, I wouldn't be heah dis mawnin'.
No, I wouldn't be a-preachin' an' a-prayin' heah.
No, suh! We is heah because we believes...
We all tryin' to belong to Yo', Lawd.
We all chillun of Gawd.
Maybe you ax me: What is a chile of Gawd?
I'll tell yo', I'll tell yo'!
We got to be humble,
We got to be meek.
Yassuh! We got tuh be like li'l chillun.

An' me, myself, I'm a witness, Lawd,
Yes, a witness to de Resurrection.
I done seed fuh myself ...
Yes, I seed Him rise
An' I seed Him good.
He rose up, 'way up, in muh soul!
'Way up! 'Way up in muh soul!

The congregation cried out in ecstasy. There were
shouts of agreement: 'I see Him rise, an' I see Him
good!' and 'Yes, Lawd!'

His soul done spring up like a grain of cawn.
You know cawn?
You done see it sprout?
Dat's me, and dat's you!
An' dat's Jesus!
We sproutin' up,
We springin' up,
Yes, sproutin' up in de springtime of de yeah!
Dat's de Resurrection of Jesus!
Sproutin' up!
Comin' back to life!
Risin' high!
Look yonder! It's gettin' daylight!
Soon yo'll see de trees, soon yo'll see de flowers!
Soon yo'll see de sunrise!
*Jesus, is dat You?*

Outside the first gray daylight was showing at the
windows, and within the church the negroes shouted
and sang. Presently, the preacher's voice was heard
again, quieter this time:

O, lemme be like Jesus,
Lemme be dressed up in white!

'Cause we know, Jesus, dat de time is come,
De time of Resurrection.
It's time fo' de first fruit to come,
De first peach, an' de first plum,
Mos' time fo' de first watermelon.
All dem fruits come hangin' on de trees,
Or bustin' from de groun',
An' we know what dat means.
It means Resurrection!
Yes, springin' up again!
We goin' tuh rise!
Oh, Angel, I want yo' to come down to earth dis mawnin' —
Come swift on de mawnin' light!
Come roll de stone from off my heart!
Roll it away, Angel, cause it's a heavy stone!

Outside the light was brighter, and the sky was
growing rosy with dawn. Inside the church the negroes
were moaning and crying and shouting aloud. As the
preacher continued the excitement grew:

Some of these days...
Trumpet goin' tuh sound!
An' Jesus is goin' tuh get up and ride de air!
He goin' tuh shout and clap His hands!
An' call us all to Resurrection.
We'll answer you, Jesus!
Heah we come!
Every tombstone will bust open!
We all goin' tuh get up!
We'll meet ouh Lawd in de middle of de air!
A fambly from heah, an' a fambly from theah!
From de river, an' from de sea!
From de woods, an' from under de trees!
*We'll meet ouh Jesus in de middle of de air,*
*An' never cry no mo'!*

The congregation was standing now, shouting aloud. In the early light Famie could see black faces streaked with tears. Many were lying on the floor before the pulpit, crying. Old Aunt Dicey, her arms lifted high, her head thrown back, cried out: 'Lawd! Please, Lawd!'

As the round, red sun mounted above the horizon the singing rose to an ecstatic, wordless melody, infinitely sweet. Women shrieked and fell to the floor. Men danced and clapped their hands. The church was a mass of swaying, gesticulating figures, shouting to the rising sun.

Famie felt Henry's arm around her, and saw that he was praying: 'Yo' so good to me, Lawd ... Lemme be worthy ...'

She knew then that he was the one person in the world that needed her.

Suddenly the shouting ended. The preacher raised his hand for silence. There was a short prayer, and, singing, the negroes marched from the church. Famie and Henry went with them.

> Ah'm goin' to meet my friends again.
> On dat great Risin' Day ...
> Ah'm goin' to meet my friends again.
> Halleloo ...

Outside there was a babble of talk. Friends greeted each other. Many intended spending the day at the

church, for there was to be another service at noon —
a service which would last until nearly twilight.

Some of the negroes were building fires under the
trees. Coffee was being dripped. Baskets were opened
and breakfasts were prepared. Little black children
had their hands full of Easter eggs, red, yellow, and
blue. Famie thought of her own church on Isle Brevelle.

Lizzie Balize, Mug and Henry-Jack and Aunt Dicey
came up to speak to Famie. And others — black men
and women that she knew only by sight — came up
to her to shake her hand and tell her that she was welcome. They looked from her face to the happy face
of Henry Tyler, understood, and accepted without
question.

Presently Henry untied the mule from the cemetery
fence and they mounted and rode off through the woods.
The sun was gilding the tree-tops, but beneath the
branches it was still dim. In the clearings, dew glittered
on grass and clover. They rode silently, not speaking
to each other, each lost in a dream, and the old mule
nibbled at depending vines.

At last the cotton-field lay before them, and far off
on the river road they saw an automobile go whizzing
by.

'Ah'll cook our dinner, Henry,' she said.

'An' after that, Ah'll come wid my wagon and move
yo' things ovah to my house.'

Mr. Guy had given the road-builders right of way

through his newly acquired land. A bridge would cross
Cane River where the Vidal house had stood for a
century. Tomorrow the men were coming to tear the
house down, and Famie was moving into Henry's
house.

Together they jogged homeward on the mule.
Blue smoke curled upward from the kitchen chimney
of the big-house at Yucca; it was nearly breakfast time.

A dilapidated surrey was approaching in the road, and
Famie, peering under her sunbonnet and around
Henry's shoulder, saw that John Javilée was driving
old Madame Aubert Rocque down to the flatboat on
the way to church. She felt her heart quicken, and
tears started to her eyes. Madame Aubert had said:
'If yo' meet me in the road, don't speak to me.'

Swathed in shawls the old woman sat with Numa's
mother on the back seat. John Javilée looked at Henry
on his mule, and recognized Famie riding behind him.
His face hardened as he flicked the reins on the back of
the roan horse. He looked full in Famie's face, then
spat over the wheel into the road.

Numa's mother turned away and put her black-
bordered handkerchief up to her eyes, but Madame
Aubert Rocque looked straight ahead. None of them
spoke to her.

Henry lifted his hat as the surrey and mule passed
in the road, and Famie bowed her head and hoped that

Henry would not know that she was crying. She tried
to stop, but it was no use.

A shining automobile stood before the gate of the
flower-garden at Yucca. Flossie and Harry Smith were
arriving for their Easter visit. Flossie stood beside the
running-board of the car, a camera in her hand.

'Oh, Harry, just look at the couple on that old white
mule! Aren't they *wonderful?* I must take their
picture...'

'Oh, come on, Flossie, it's just some niggers on their
way home from church.'

But Flossie was signaling Henry Tyler to stop: 'Oh,
please wait. I want to take your *picture*. Yes, turn the
mule around a little and ask your wife to look at me...
What's the matter, is she shy? Lift up your head, I
can't see your face for that sunbonnet... Well, never
mind, you'll look coy with your head down. Maybe it
will be *better* that way, more natural. Now, boy, you
smile. Don't look so *solemn*. Harry, give him a dime,
won't you? There, I've *got* it. But I never did see the
woman's face.'

'Come on, Flossie, put the camera away and let's go in.'

'Well, of course I'm going in. You didn't think I was
going to stay out here in the *road* all day. Harry, I'll
bet I've got the *grandest* picture. They were so *typical*.
You know, Harry, I always say that niggers are the
*happiest* people. Not a care in the world.'